PRAISE FOR
HAILEY PIPER

"One of the most powerful rising voices in genre fiction."
– *Paste Magazine*

"[Piper's] fiction is remarkable in its range." - *Esquire*

"Delightfully fucked-up and tremendously imaginative."
– *Vulture*

"Glorious and visceral." - Chuck Wendig, *New York Times* Bestselling author of *Wanderers*

"Fresh, fantastic." - Josh Malerman, *New York Times* Bestselling author of *Bird Box*

"Thrillingly original." - Rachel Harrison, *USA Today* Bestselling author of *Black Sheep*

ALSO BY HAILEY PIPER

CRANBERRY COVE

COVE

HAILEY PIPER

Bad Hand Books
www.badhandbooks.com

FOREWORD IS FOREARMED

I don't set out to shock anyone. That's never been my way. There are the feelings and thoughts I want to explore and express, and there's the story that lets me do it. Sometimes, the story shocks, but that's incidental. I can't decide that. We all keep colliding with each other, and life comes out of those interactions, but my outlook is never "see if you can handle *this*" and then throwing a live wire at you. At most, there is a book.

But I also don't set out to reassure. The only thing I can assure you of is that there will be wonderful and terrible people in your life, and that sometimes you will confuse the two, and sometimes they will be the same person, and sometimes they'll surprise you.

This is a laborious way of saying, this is a bleak book. It might not be for you. I write lots of different kinds of stories, set in cities, caverns, made-up lands, outer space, and it would be surprising for all of them to fit any one particular reader. Yes, this one involves hauntings and creepy places, subjects you might expect of me, but it also involves discussions and confrontations with abuse, sexual harassment, and assault. I'm grateful to Doug Murano for lending book space to this warning, Lynne Hansen for giving the book a stunning and appropriate cover, and my wife J for encouraging the story to be told.

That story only reaches you if you choose to read it, and that is entirely up to you. Cranberry Cove awaits.

Hailey Piper
January 2024

CRANBERRY COVE

ONE: ARRIVAL

C ranberry Cove. The name gave Emberly Hale visions of an enormous gored-out cranberry seated on the desolate corner of Washington Avenue and Mayhew Street, its entrance a chewed-away cavern of fruit guts and scarlet intestines.

She never came to this side of town, hardly anyone did anymore, where plywood coated the windows and glass littered the sidewalk. No reason to see what Cranberry Cove really looked like until today.

As Conner Bohme parked his gray Mazda at the opposite corner's curb, Emberly took in the full and disappointing view through the windshield. Cranberry Cove was a corner hotel, spreading along either sidewalk with *Cranberry* jutting in blocky vertical letters down to the horizontal *Cove* above the gaping entrance. It wore a similar grayed-over atmosphere as its neighboring businesses and apartments, clinical depression having taken physical form in their brick and mortar and grime. Planks covered the lobby windows, but no one had bothered to board up the higher floors. If ghosts rented spectral rooms, they would get the same high view as the living visitors before them, only upon a more decayed side of town than back in the hotel's glory days.

Conner unlatched himself from the car first and slammed the driver's door harder than he needed. Emberly slipped out after him from the passenger side. They both stared at the hotel, and it stared right back.

"What the hell made our dear prince come here?" Conner said, shaking his head.

"It's been abandoned since the '70s," Emberly said. "Duke probably thought no one would bother him, Kristof, or Tyrone's guys while they showed product and talked out a deal."

More than anything, Duke was too green, and he had seen too many movies. He was the type to believe professional arrangements took place in shitholes like Cranberry Cove, and now his rudimentary blurring between cinema and life meant Emberly and Conner had to march down here, putting truth to celluloid fantasy. Life would imitate film when it should have been the other way around.

But then, wasn't Emberly putting the blame on Duke for coming here? She bit her tongue, and the pain derailed that train of thought.

Conner scratched his arm where a nicotine patch hid beneath his jacket. Once upon a time, they both wore denim and street clothes to these types of situations. Since Emberly's wardrobe change toward dark blue jacket dresses like the one she wore over her tall pale form today, Conner had taken to fitting a black suit and tie over his brawny figure. Each carried themselves with professional airs these days, as if they were better people than before. Pretending helped.

"It's ridiculous," Conner muttered, starting toward the Mazda's trunk. "His father has fingers in too many establishments for the prince to bother with this ancient gutter of a place."

"He's twenty-two," Emberly said, following him. Her wavy chestnut hair stroked her shoulders in the wind. "He couldn't have known the Cove's reputation."

"Shouldn't matter." Conner smoothed short dark hair from his boxy pinkish face and popped the trunk. "Neither of us are that old, either, but we know better."

His math checked out. Cranberry Cove shut down over fifty years ago, and were the man responsible for its poor fortune and worse reputation still skulking its halls, he'd have to be in his seventies or eighties by now, or older. No way the past should have mattered.

And yet what could the past do besides haunt the present?

Emberly glanced beyond the open trunk toward the hotel's naked windows, free to glare down on the intersection without eyelids of wood, and in some cases without curtains. Cranberry Cove kept watch.

"Ricard wasn't clear on his directive, was he?" Conner asked. "He can't expect the guy to be hanging around."

Did Conner mean the guy from decades ago? Or did he mean the guy who'd hurt Duke Morrison, eldest son of their employer Ricard Morrison and heir to his many businesses, legitimate or otherwise?

Emberly guessed it didn't matter. They had the means to deal with either. She reached into the open trunk and slipped a black semi-automatic shotgun into her arms, where it clacked against the brass buttons of her jacket dress. Its metal was warm in her hands, baked by summer heat caught in the car trunk.

Conner lifted the shotgun's identical lover, slammed the trunk shut, and led Emberly toward the opposite street corner.

The hotel had stood abandoned only five decades, and yet a primordial pit opened at its front, where living creatures fell into nests of sharp nails and vicious teeth.

"We'll find out who did it." Emberly nudged her shotgun muzzle against the ajar lobby door, its hinges squeaking in the wind. "Or who didn't. Look for clues. Rule out Tyrone's people so Ricard won't have to make war."

Conner let his shotgun dangle as if swinging a small child back and forth. "Like we're fucking cops?"

"Not at all," Emberly said, smiling with her back to the door. "We're expected to get results."

Conner coughed a laugh and then gestured ahead. "Ladies first."

TWO: INSIDE

Strips of ceiling plaster drooped in great boneless fingers across the lobby. Dust and garbage coated a tipped-over trolley, the check-in desk, and the pots of long-dead plants. The broad gray-brown rug made *squish–squish* noises underfoot. Emberly smelled mildew and old clothes, but her imagination danced with the hotel's name, suggesting a cranberry scent too. Summer heat thickened the air.

"There could be homeless snuggling up in the rooms," Conner said. "Or in the walls."

The outdoor light seeped milky through grime-caked glass into the lobby, around rusty-nailed planks and moldering curtains. A breath of radiant sunshine lit the top of the main stairway, suggesting an open room upstairs with an uncovered window. It was almost hopeful.

But between the stairs rising from the lobby and the stairs running down from the second floor, a thick shadow blanketed the stairway landing.

Emberly stared into it, waiting for her eyes to

make out the corner, a pattern on the wall, anything. It remained an unfading oily cloud.

Conner kicked at a soggy patch of wall. "Should've torn this place down."

"It'll have its day," Emberly said, heading for the check-in desk.

"Sure," Conner said. "Somebody'll give a shit about this patch of town for a change, feed the whole thing to a herd of bulldozers, and stick up a condo nobody can afford to live in. Exactly as abandoned as it is now."

Emberly couldn't argue with him; she'd seen those exact steps of progress play out too many times in too many places. She craned her neck over the check-in desk. No computers, no touchscreen registration, only empty cubbies where moldering logbooks must have been kept. Everything here was analog and decayed.

A clumsy thud drew her eyes again to the stairway, where Conner pressed a shoe on the lowest step. The unseen landing above taunted with hairy darkness.

"You don't want to check the pool's changing room?" Emberly asked. "Dining hall?"

"It didn't happen down here." Conner chinned up the stairs and then mimicked with his shotgun muzzle. "It happened up there."

Emberly elbowed the check-in desk countertop, as if it would cough up answers at a touch, and then followed Conner to the stairs. An argument seemed pointless. He'd driven out on Ricard's order, no reconnaissance or caution. Emberly had at least skimmed a news article first.

She hadn't expected much for a hotel abandoned long before the internet could properly digitize its every movement. The one article she had bothered to read dispelled any notion of Cranberry Cove as a haunted hotel in the classic sense of ghosts, specters, and the like, only to be notoriously unsafe for what little attention it still gained, with barely a whisper about the alleged crimes of yesteryear.

Alleged being the article's word, and a bullshit one. That anyone had reported at all seemed a miracle, and those who had done so wouldn't have gained anything by inventing such stories. While Emberly refused to spend hours poring over microfiche in the local library, she guessed any newspapers from the time of the hotel's downfall had sandwiched the true wording of the crimes into conveniently obscuring language.

It hadn't helped. Even in the days before business social media accounts and Yelp reviews, word of mouth must have spread far enough to tarnish the hotel's reputation until the owners finally shut it down. Whether they meant to do so briefly or forever, the latter became Cranberry Cove's future.

That did not erase the reputation. It lingered across time, same as the hotel itself.

"There's no cursed room in particular," Emberly called up the stairs. "From what I read, it happened in different rooms back in the day."

"I don't care about back in the day," Conner said, a shrug in his tone. "I care about yesterday. And now."

He reached the landing between lobby and second floor, and his details and shape vanished as if black curtains now draped around him. Only the sheen of his shotgun muzzle told Emberly he stood above her.

The shotgun aimed up. "How far does it go?" the dark landing asked in Conner's voice.

"Seven floors, for good luck," Emberly said. She climbed in slow steps. "It was only men. The ones who reported it."

"I know that much from its reputation."

"Shouldn't I take point then?" Emberly reached the landing, enclosing herself in darkness with Conner.

"It doesn't matter," Conner said. "Seven floors, ten rooms each? We'll have to split up if we don't find anything where the prince—where it happened."

He emerged from the landing onto the next flight of stairs, and Emberly hurried behind him. They found a sister darkness at the far end of the second floor, but it broke into clear light where Room 2A's door hung wide open. Gray daylight clawed across the mottled carpet at the top of the stairs. Emberly almost felt it beckon. The other doors stood shut tight, only meager lines of light breaching their undersides.

Duke hadn't sat alone in Room 2A at first. He'd waited with Kristof O'Keefe, another of Ricard Morrison's crew, for Tyrone's representatives to show up. To hear Kristof tell it, he left the room to check on the sound of someone knocking on a hard surface. Polite, like room service requesting entry.

Might've been Tyrone's guys, he'd said.

But it wasn't room service or somebody working for Tyrone. As far as anyone knew, no one from Tyrone's end had bothered to show up on his behalf and meet with Duke to examine the sampling of his father's arsenal. Maybe they had mixed up the address, or maybe they had seen the look of Cranberry Cove and skittered off with common sense tucked behind their teeth.

Tyrone's men or not, someone had found Duke alone in 2A. Someone had hurt him.

The room was any other hotel hole. A bathroom opened to the right of the door, and a small dresser sat across from the twin beds. Someone had long ago swiped the boxy old television from its top, but they'd left the indent lines in the wood behind. A dust-coated blue lamp perched atop the nightstand between beds, free of lightbulb and lampshade. The ceiling light hung dark. Balls of crumpled newspaper, candy wrappers, and trash-filled plastic bags littered the floor, suggesting someone had squatted here more recently than the hotel's closing in the '70s. Both beds stretched naked of bedding, but a briefcase sat atop the nearest.

Kristof had left the product sample behind when he helped Duke get away. Neither said whether they'd seen anyone else.

"It took three reports to bring Cranberry Cove to its knees," Emberly said. "Nobody wanted to stay after that."

"Not even women?" Conner flicked open the bed-top briefcase, where pieces of a scoped long-range rifle waited to be assembled. "If it was only men involved."

"*If* is the key word. Who could trust that distinction would stay the case?" Emberly peeked over Conner's shoulder—every piece of the rifle remained in its functionless solitude. "Incidents like those don't get reported all the time, from anyone, but especially men. Look at Duke. We only know because Ricard told us. People might've kept firm secrets back then, like they do now."

"Meaning there could've been women, too." Conner shut the briefcase with a metal *tick*. "We'll take this with us."

Emberly's nod led her gaze to a row of red dots along the mattress. "Likely there were more than three men back then. Out of the whole, what percentage would report at all?"

"Sure you want to brave this place?" Conner asked, pacing toward the door. "I can handle it alone."

Emberly bit her cheeks not to laugh. Conner's unflinching bravado, no matter where they went, could be both insulting and hilarious. If there was anything here to find, he wouldn't be the one to find it. His mind was all thumbs.

"I can take it." Emberly tried to make this statement

co-exist with her longing glances at 2A's entrance. "I'd do anything for Ricard."

"So would I," Conner said. "I'm not afraid some freak will come at me, but this place is a ghost town, and I'm no believer in ghosts, which means something else is likely to crawl around. Something worse."

Conner neared the door, shotgun in one hand, briefcase in the other. He eyed the bathroom, a dark place that rejected the generosity of the main room's daylight.

He then turned back and offered a gentle smile. "If you're scared—I mean, everything with this guy, let's say he's the same one? He'd take one look and know you're a woman. But if he knew about your past, how you showed yourself then, he might misunderstand. We're the enlightened kind, but you never can tell. It's not always like it is with Ricard. Not all good ones."

"Ricard paid for everything," Emberly said. "Everything. I owe him."

"I'm trying to look out for you," Conner said.

Emberly chuckled, flashing her teeth. "I appreciate your sexist chivalry is trans inclusive." But she meant it a little, annoying or not.

"I'm one of the good ones, too; you know that." Conner raised both shotgun and briefcase in surrender, and then he laid the briefcase in the hallway and turned again to the room. "Fine, fine. Let's get this sorted."

They kicked through the floor trash, keeping watch for odd footprints, dropped identification, a scrap of too-nice clothing. Any hint as to what person might have slipped into this room while Duke Morrison should have sat alone, playing a game on his phone to calm his nerves. The slightest clue as to who exactly had held him down and then violated him.

Emberly peeked into the bathroom and toggled the light switch, but it remained a black hole in the wall until she held up her phone and tapped on its flashlight app.

Grime-coated tiles stretched over the chipped and crumbling floor. The sink remained standing, its basin coated in gray dust beneath a broken mirror. A toilet haunted the far side of the bathroom, across from a dangling shower curtain. It looked too new for the rest of the room.

Emberly treaded inside, leaving shoe prints on the tiles, and shoved the curtain aside. She half-expected to find a dead body stashed in the porcelain tub, its edges cracked and moldy, but she found only a layer of yellow scum. Not even insects had taken advantage of the moist cold to lay their eggs or crawl in their dark kingdom.

"How are we supposed to tell a damn thing?" Conner asked. "There's so much garbage. Pretty sure raccoons were living here at some point."

Emberly retreated from the bathroom and eyed Room 2A for signs of raccoon paw prints. Had they been the source of whatever knocking noise Kristof had heard? Vermin in the walls seemed a given for an abandoned hotel, but without people, Emberly doubted animals found much to eat here, aside from each other.

Maybe Kristof had followed the sounds of a ghost.

"There were disappearances, too," Emberly said, opening the nightstand. A rotted *Holy Bible* stared up at her before she shut the little drawer. "Not many, but they made a bigger buzz than the assault reports, helped those fall through the journalistic cracks. The difference couldn't save Cranberry Cove."

"A people-eating hotel," Conner said. "That kind of urban legend might make a good tourist trap. Until it turned out true."

He had a point. For all Emberly knew, travelers had wandered this way over the past few decades, seeking adventure, mystery, or a tall tale of their own, only to never be heard from again. Their cars might have lined Washington Avenue or Mayhew Street until the city towed them or street kids stripped them to automobile skeletons and then nothingness. No evidence they were here, no remains to send home.

Gone from all knowledge, with Cranberry Cove the last place they would ever see on Earth.

Conner strode past the bathroom and across the second-floor hallway, where he tried the door to Room 2B. Its wood groaned, but the door held fast.

"They still used toothy keys instead of keycards, huh?" Conner bent as if to peer through the keyhole.

"But they didn't leave the keys behind. Unless they hid them."

He vanished from 2A's view as his footsteps slid down the hall. Another door complained beneath his touch. Emberly listened as he tested the doors of 2C, 2D, 2E. Finding keys might have been a good reason to properly search the lobby before climbing up here, but if the doors were locked and the keys awaited below, unlikely Emberly or Conner would find anyone or anything within these rooms.

Duke had found an already-open door and waited dutifully on one of the beds. Empty-headed green boy with his head full of crime dramas and action movies. He should have known better, being his father's son, but few twenty-two-year-olds valued wisdom.

How long did he sit here before the wrong meeting came to find him?

And which meeting? With one of Tyrone's people, or a complete outsider, or the man from the '70s who'd brought Cranberry Cove to its knees? Emberly didn't know. Had it been her choice, she wouldn't have set foot in this seedy grave of visitations past. Tyrone's people must have thought the same, and she needed to rule them out. No one wanted a street war.

Emberly paused over one naked mattress, attention fixed on its tiny red dots. Blood would have browned by now, like a skinned apple. The red had to be paint, or candle wax, or—

Knock-knock-knock.

Emberly's ear twitched at the noise. She glanced back over the empty room and wiped at her neck, where sweat dotted her skin. The air was still and smelled of decay.

"Conner?" Emberly called. "Is that you?"

He didn't answer. She listened to another door resist his hand, farther away now, another curse under his breath. If his whisper of "Shitting hell" could reach down the hall, so could his knocking on one of the doors. Each room had one way in, one way out, unless you counted the window for a permanent check-out. Where else could the noise have come from?

Knock-knock-knock.

There it was again. What could it be—raccoons? Some other animal in the walls? The noise was gentle, almost polite. Emberly could imagine a visitor of decades past sitting on this bed, oblivious to its red dots through sheets and bedding. They would hear the knock, assume room service, and welcome the knocker. Had a hotel guest of yesteryear ever opened their room door to find no one standing in the hall?

Except everyone loved to tell ghost stories, and no one loved to talk about the kind of wrong done in Cranberry Cove. That Emberly had heard about the assaults and not a word on phantoms suggested there were no ghost stories, and there likely were no ghosts.

The sound had to have a physical source. Emberly turned to the bed again, ready to listen for the next series of knocks.

She heard nothing before the bony weight slammed against her back.

Her shoes left the cluttered floor as she sprawled hard onto the bed, smacking her face and chest against the mattress. One of her hands splayed to the side. The other gripped her shotgun, its muzzle pointing at the next bed, another empty place. She had no way to turn around and aim when a breastbone jammed hard between her shoulder blades and another hand, a stranger's hand, pinned her shooting arm. The safety was still on, too.

She turned her head, trying to look at the fingers holding her limb, but the weight sank tight against her neck at a painful angle, keeping her head from moving. Hot breath slid across one ear.

"Conner!" Emberly's shriek was meek, awkward, hateful.

She tried to jerk back, but this body kept her pinned in place. That hot breath broke into short, wet gasps, the fevered snuffling of an animal rooting against her hair, behind her ear, down the sides of her jacket dress. Curious fingers wedged beneath her pinned torso and tested at the brass buttons.

"Conner!" she shouted again, voice cracking.

Distant footsteps pounded over a mottled rug. She wanted to scream for Conner to be careful, that the collapsing ceiling below warned of a thin floor, but her concern was a tiny caged animal beneath her furious heart and pulsing fear.

Her arms tensed, meaning to force her up from the bed.

Another hand jammed her face hard into the mattress. She sucked in breaths choked by bedded rot and calcified sweat. The world stilled around her, the figure at her back tensing so hard that she could scarcely twitch in place. The echoes of Conner's thunderous approach quieted around her.

Hot breath withdrew from her body. The figure quit snuffling and leaned harder against her head, a jaw prodding into her skull. Fingers squeezed at her limbs and scalp.

And then a vicious croaking voice whispered in her ear. "Summoner. Grant. Where?"

Footsteps stormed toward 2A's doorway as the weight climbed from Emberly's back. She dragged her shotgun from across the bed into both hands, switched the safety off, pumped once, and flopped over.

Where Conner filled 2A's hall.

They both aimed at each other on instinct and then turned their guns away. Emberly pointed her shotgun at the bed where she'd been pressed down, and then the next bed, the dresser, the windows.

The room was empty. No sign of anyone.

Conner rushed into the bathroom, jammed an elbow at the dead light switch, and then his phone's flashlight lit up the doorframe. A cabinet door screeched and clacked. Shower curtain rings hissed over a rod. He appeared between the hall and bathroom doorway a moment later, mouth agape, brow furrowed.

Emberly probably looked the same. She couldn't mouth a question, but she hoped it was obvious on her face. *Who? Where?*

"There's nobody," Conner said, aiming his shotgun every which way. "Nobody."

THREE: OKAY

Emberly lost track of how many times she had to tell Conner she wasn't hurt. Every word was a strange contradiction. *Nothing happened*, she could say, and yet something had. And something else, almost.

Maybe. She wasn't sure. It wasn't nothing, and yet it kind of was, and she didn't know how to sort out those polar opposites. Especially with the frequent interruptions.

"You're okay?" Conner asked. Emberly had lost track of how many times he'd asked that, too.

She could only nod as they stepped into Shipley's Pub. Did Ricard own the property or merely lease the land? Emberly couldn't remember, but here was the only place she wanted to be right now. The pub's insides echoed a serene log cabin merged with a bar. The air gathered the sounds of pool sticks sliding from the wall or glass mugs clinking, and it clouded with the familiar scents of alcohol, leather seating, and the occasional waft of a sweet cigar whenever Minerva came in from one of her smoke breaks.

Conner rubbed where his nicotine patch hid as he led the way to the back of the pub, their favorite booth. Minerva swept by with menus and water and a wink for Conner. He ordered a Guinness, and Emberly asked for a vodka martini.

For a brief moment, the evening seemed gentle, like the day might let Emberly go.

And then Conner asked again if she was okay, a question that cut through the aural landscape of billiards games and dull conversational rumble. His expression was concerned, insistent. Like he expected a different answer this time.

Emberly thought of smashing her water glass against the edge of the table and cutting a line down his cheek so she could ask if he was okay, over and over, make it even between them. She instead slid her the glass back and forth, its ice murmuring famous last words against a slow and melty transformation. Summer slid warm breath into the pub each time its front door opened.

"Ricard doesn't respect me anymore," Emberly said. "Because you're too protective."

"I'm not protective enough," Conner said. "If I had been, I'd have—" He shot a finger gun across the table, his hollow effort at humor.

"Hm." Emberly thought again of cutting him. She instead crunched an ice chip between her molars and thought of Ricard. "The nerve of him."

Minerva swept by a second time, setting down

small napkins and the drinks. Conner told her they would need a minute, and she patted his arm with a smile.

Emberly tried to look at the menu, but her head weighed into her hands. Her skull had grown heavy over the course of the afternoon, full of responsibilities and failures and loose ends yet untied.

Recounting the events at the abandoned hotel to Ricard an hour ago had scraped glass shards down her nerves. Worse than that, she and Conner had returned to him empty-handed. Not that she didn't tell him what had happened to some degree, but even if he believed her, he had no reason to assume there was any connection between her mystery nobody and the incident with his son in Room 2A of Cranberry Cove.

Which meant Ricard would press harder at Tyrone's people. He would demand retribution, satisfaction, revenge—the works. He would bring war to the streets.

Emberly was in no position to ask him questions or make demands, but she desperately wanted him to know how much worse a situation a parent could find themselves in when facing a place like Cranberry Cove. It had a history of hurting people, yes, but it also had a history of swallowing them whole.

Didn't Ricard understand he could have lost his son entirely? Duke could have sat on that bed while Kristof wandered off, except instead of finding Duke when he returned, there could have been a man-shaped hole in the world, already filled with stale air and dust motes. The walls could have eaten Duke and never explained a thing.

But society acted like murder was the best outcome when someone came after you. Easier for everyone else if you became the tidy and honored deceased, not a voice speaking of travesty that no one wanted to hear.

Easier to choose silence. Play dead. Make no one understand what had happened to you.

Conner's hard sigh drew Emberly from her thoughts. Neither of them had glanced at their menus. Conner had heard every word Emberly said to Ricard, but he hadn't voiced much opinion about it. Only asked if she was okay, again and again.

"Go on." Emberly chinned at him. "Tell me your thoughts."

"Might seem unfair, but Ricard has something of a point?" Conner said, his pitch rising at the last word, reluctant to assert that opinion too firmly in case Emberly took offense. "If it'd been me in that room when the guy—"

"Thing," Emberly cut in. One fingernail scratched down her water glass, and then she sipped her martini.

"Right, when the guy-thing came out." Conner swept a palm over the small table. "It wouldn't have gone that way. I would've made sure of it."

Emberly studied Conner's earnest eyes and steady hands for his telltale bravado, but every inch of him believed the words out of his mouth. No posturing, full confidence. Like he lived in a different world, set a little to the left of the real one.

For a big man, he could be such a boy. And a fool.

"Conner?" Emberly's tone filled with gentle curiosity as she leaned over the table. "You've never been overpowered before, have you?"

"When I was a kid, sure," Conner said, half-shrugging one mountainous shoulder. "Penbrook Park was like that. Same with my parents, especially my dad. But not these days."

"You don't ever think about it?" Emberly asked. "Don't you ever consider what it would be like to lose all control under someone else?"

"I get into fights to win them." Conner tapped his beer bottle against the table twice for emphasis. "Getting beat down is one thing, but stuck under somebody's mercy? That's more a womanly thing. No offense."

Emberly wanted to shake him. She kept her tone light. "But the other guy thinks the same."

Conner screwed up his face. "He what?"

"The other guy," Emberly said. "He thinks being overpowered is a womanly concern, too, same as you. He's not considering it when he's against you, either. Neither of you has the slightest idea how it feels, even in your imagination, even though it could happen to either of you. For women, it's always what she wore, where she walked, who she was with, how much she drank or smoked or snorted, how much did she really not want it, quantifiers and qualifiers until the end of time. It's always possible. For men, it's unspeakable. Unthinkable."

"Can't happen, so it didn't?" Conner asked.

"There's a ridiculous logic to it, don't you think?" Emberly gave the table a sullen look. "Unspoken, unthought. When it comes to Cranberry Cove, it's shocking even three reports surfaced back then."

"Is it?" Conner's mind worked this over, the effort obvious in his creased forehead. He then shuddered against the booth seat and waved a meaty hand in dismissal. "What the hell do you know? Look, I get that those meds have made your muscles go soppy, but for me? Nothing like that. Couldn't be further from the case."

His fingers drummed up and down the table. He was searching for another thought, another project, anything to drag his attention from dredged-up discomfort.

Emberly's hand flinched, eager to reach over, take one of his, comfort him. That was the trade, right? Man protects, woman comforts. Maybe her non-binary friends were free of societal expectation so long as society ignored them. She hadn't entirely understood what she was stepping into when her transition began, only Ricard's promise that she would have the entire crew's due understanding and support.

True to his word, everyone saw her as the woman she was. With all the casual disrespect that entailed.

Conner's finger-drumming burst into a palm slapping the table. "Fucking hell, Em. Ricard's threatening war with Tyrone, and we're tasked to find answers or else, meanwhile you're wasting everyone's time and patience saying the goddamn boogeyman came out of the walls and went devil-shit on the prince himself."

Emberly kept her tone flat. "I'm not making light of this."

"Me neither," Conner said, easing up. "I'm frustrated."

"Then can you quit calling Duke that goofy nickname?" Emberly asked. "He might not even know what found him. You wouldn't know, either."

"Because I don't believe in the boogeyman, or the devil, none of that shit." Conner glared across the table, at his menu. His eyes screwed up, like he'd forgotten how to read, as if the pressure of Minerva's eventual return to take their orders had made him anxious.

Emberly knew better. His anxiety had a more sinister source.

"But Em," Conner said, lifting his eyes to her. "I believe you. There was somebody in that room, and there's no way he should've slipped by me. Couldn't happen, so it didn't, but I know for a fact it did. What I don't know is what to do with that contradiction. I'm just sorry for it."

"It wasn't on you to handle." Emberly sipped her drink. "Things happen."

"But they shouldn't." Conner reached across the table and took her hand in his. "I should've been there."

She let Conner hold on, her way of comforting him that he was the stronger of the two, which was true, and that he could watch out for her. That part, she was less certain about.

But for as much as Ricard's dismissal and Conner's delusions of knighthood sometimes shrank her down, gender expectations might have spared her today. Only men had reported mysterious assaults at Cranberry Cove. Far as anyone knew, only men had disappeared there.

This deep in the evening, she could smell her own body odor, mixed with everyone else at the pub, and she remembered the guy-thing sniffing at her hair, her clothes, felt its head pressed at her sides. She could almost feel it now.

Conner eyed her expression. "Your turn. Tell me your thoughts."

"I wonder what Duke felt," Emberly said. "What he saw."

"He told Ricard," Conner said. "Ricard told us. We got the story as we need it."

"All we know is, he was alone, and someone attacked him." Emberly drew her hand back to her side of the table. "We don't know if he—we don't know anything really."

She thought again of that pressure at her back, the *inspection* for lack of a better word. Like the guy-thing was looking for something. Or someone.

Summoner. Grant. Where?

"That cluelessness," Emberly went on. "The reason you don't expect a threat. That might be how it went down for Duke."

"I don't follow," Conner said.

"The guy-thing." Emberly leaned deeper into the table and lowered her voice. She could hear Minerva coming their way again. "What if it was looking for a man? And only a man? Same as the Cove's old incidents and disappearances."

Conner stared thoughtfully again. "Why you then? Even if your creeper was a hateful little shit, how's it likely to make that mistake? Why not come for me?"

Emberly had no answer. Under the grip of a hungry animal, what exactly had saved her? Hair length? Scent and hormones? Skin texture? Her choice of dress over suit? The thirteen-month absence of penis and testicles between her legs? She couldn't guess how the guy-thing chose its targets, but her imagination grabbed at every possibility to differentiate herself from this Summoner Grant it had come looking for.

And there was a sick, subtle relief, too, a semblance of euphoria and validation within the guy-thing's distaste toward her.

She hated herself for it.

FOUR: THE STORM

That night, a summer storm washed into town moments before Emberly stepped into the shower. Gentle thunder rumbled overhead as she slid the glass door aside, and the sound of rain pattering her apartment windows melted into the rhythm of the showerhead pouring water down on her. She stayed in too long, letting the hot water redden her skin, but it was a purifying sensation. Any trace of Cranberry Cove would spatter on the shower floor and then slip down the drain.

She had hoped the storm would end by the time she finished, but the rain's percussion went on beating the windows and rooftop, and her lights flickered while she was drying off. Overworked air conditioners were already taxing the area's grid without a storm to challenge it too.

Emberly lit preemptive candles on the coffee table in the living room, the kitchen island's countertop, beside the bathroom sink, and on her bedroom vanity before she finished drying off and getting into a loose tank top and summer shorts. If the storm brought a blackout, she was ready.

She didn't want too much darkness tonight.

"Fucking Cranberry Cove," she whispered, and then laughed to herself and started brushing her hair.

The storm rumbled a wordless answer. Emberly almost wished she had someone else here tonight besides the weather, but she was in the habit of bringing bad decisions home, and she especially hadn't trusted herself not to do that tonight.

She found her hands shaking as she set the hairbrush down on the vanity, inches from one glowing candle. Her reflection stretched up the glass, a damp, somber image. She pressed her hands to her cheeks and smushed the flesh around as if reshaping clay, but she wasn't sure what she meant to see. The skin only hugged at her jaw and cheekbones. There were no secrets here, not even visible scars. Unless Ricard called or texted, Emberly was off from work until tomorrow. There was no reason to think about the day anymore.

"So what the hell's bothering you?" she asked the mirror. Her hands dropped to the vanity. "Figure it out."

The lights went out, leaving her with the mirror and the candle. Her reflection lingered in the glass, but the dancing light and the new darkness shifted its character to mere suggestions of shape and not the whole of herself. She was only portions of a woman surfacing into the candlelight.

Anything could lurk in that darkness behind her, especially in the backwards world of the glass.

Light rushed in again, and Emberly tore herself from the vanity. She grabbed her phone from the nightstand and headed into the living room, where there were no reflections except the dark television screen. It glowed with brief blue light before she switched it to stream a long-ended sitcom. The show offered background images without soul or purpose. Something harmless she could glance toward if she needed reassurance, so long as the power didn't go out again.

She stretched across the couch beneath the flickering glow. Her phone's glare made her eyes ache a little—she was up too late already—but the TV and candles offered enough light to keep back the boogeyman. The one she'd imagined, so said the men in her life.

Ricard's orders were for Emberly to stay away from Cranberry Cove. He would probably tell her to keep out of the inevitable street war, too. How long until he decided she had no further use in his organization?

She thumbed over her phone screen and began scrolling for any relevant information about the derelict hotel. With the right solution, she could prove her ongoing usefulness, like she always had, and show Ricard there was no need to make war with Tyrone.

The immediate results were not hopeful. Emberly's earlier reconnaissance had stuck to one brief article, but she found little better in a scant search for news items on Cranberry Cove. That area's abandoned buildings served journalism better as a footnote or background detail to more recent troubles. Who cared about a hotel left to rot for the past few decades when there were nearby properties ripe for gentrification?

Emberly found plenty of those kinds of news stories. Closed markets, forgotten arcades, the kinds of places that malls had made obsolete before the internet had given malls a taste of their own medicine. Nowadays, the surrounding run-down buildings offered havens for "junkies and vagrants," one progress-obsessed article's sneering terminology for the local street kids with nowhere else to go.

If Cranberry Cove came up at all, it was an offhand remark about how those locals would typically steer clear of the abandoned hotel. How they advised others to do the same.

Like they knew.

What would someone learn by pressing such street kids? Conner might find out, were he to return to that area. Emberly could technically join him for such an interrogation series so long as she didn't break Ricard's command to stay out of Cranberry Cove.

But that would mean following the letter of Ricard's command and not the intent. He would be disappointed in such childish mincing of words. No, he meant for her to avoid Cranberry Cove, the intersection of Washington Avenue and Mayhew Street, and everything within throwing distance, as if she were a fragile doll, her porcelain likely to shatter were she to hit the pavement the wrong way.

Emberly swiped from her news tab to her search bar and added more specific phrases beyond *Cranberry Cove*. Such as *Missing. Assailant. Sexual assault.*

Links to a handful of true crime podcasts flickered down her phone screen. There weren't many. This genre of audio program seemed more fixated on dead women than assaulted and vanished men. Women were the expected vessels for pain, and as far as the record showed, no women had been harmed at Cranberry Cove. That in itself was usual.

But the strange history of the abandoned hotel had not gone entirely unnoticed.

Emberly paused at a link to *Cold Case Journeys, Episode 106: Our Night at Cranberry Cove.*

Someone had spent a night there? She couldn't imagine it. The building had an ominous air even in the stifling light of day. Its weight had to be oppressive in the night.

That wasn't the impression she got from clicking on the link and listening to the episode as she closed her eyes. There were two hosts, Vivian and Stephanie, and they kept in good spirits. The podcast almost seemed to have a jovial tone, and Emberly wondered if that was common for every *Cold Case Journeys* episode, or perhaps true crime podcasts in general. She had no idea. She saw enough crime in her work without hunting it in her spare time.

The episode went over how Vivian and Stephanie had learned of the '70s disappearances. Their research echoed Emberly's. Only men had gone missing, same as the assault cases, though the hosts focused on the disappearances, more prosperous ground for speculation, listing names of those who had checked in to the hotel and hadn't checked out. One of them made a crass joke about cockroaches.

Emberly began to drift off as the two talked over scouting the location, assessing it to be a sturdy and empty enough structure for them to spend the night. They had to set up sleeping bags, ready themselves in case someone else noticed their presence. They'd been prepared for their trip, more than Emberly would have expected.

She was midway toward the edges of a dream when a familiar description slid into her ears and forced her awake again.

"—like the walls groaning against each other, going *knock-knock-knock*," one of the hosts said. Likely Stephanie.

Emberly opened her eyes to the flickering television. She could have said nearly the same to Ricard today. A rhythmic trio of knocking, but she would swear it wasn't caused by the walls. More like something inside those walls.

"And then in the middle of the night," Stephanie went on. "I think it was an animal walking over the sleeping bag. It came sniffing at me, like it was looking for food, but it felt big. Like a dog maybe. Oh, I need to get more specific. Like a big dog, not a cute little poodle."

"No, I get you," Vivian said.

"And you don't remember, right?" Stephanie asked.

"I slept right through it." Vivian chuckled, her voice slightly distorting in her microphone. "But I remember you flicking on the lantern. There was—"

"Nothing."

"Yeah, nothing."

Stephanie gave a nervous laugh. "We spent all that time checking for people but didn't even consider stray dogs? I never thought there'd be wildlife in there."

"Me neither," Vivian said. "I am not outdoorsy enough for Cranberry Cove."

Emberly shut off the podcast and sat up on the couch. That was no animal at the hotel today, but she changed her search again out of morbid curiosity and a hope she might cross paths with some unexpected solution. *Cranberry Cove animal attack.*

Nothing of value. Of course. Unless the abandoned hotel had sent her stumbling into a *Who Framed Roger Rabbit?* type of world, there were no animals that could ask in her ear, *Summoner. Grant. Where?* It would take a parrot or mynah bird as big as she was to weigh on her back like that.

She shuddered out of the memory and looked to her phone for guidance again. It seemed a useless hunk of plastic and circuitry in her hand. She thought of searching for something else. *Boogeyman.* Or *devil.*

But she heard Conner in her head, finishing out his trifecta, *none of that shit*, and closed the browser tabs, let her phone go dark, and dropped it onto the coffee table beside a flickering scented candle. Any more searching tonight and she would give herself a headache. She pawed for the remote and shut off the television, too.

Darkness encircled the living room except where the candle flames danced at its center. She slid her feet to the carpet and watched the tiny fires.

There was another avenue she could pursue, more concrete than running web searches for phantoms and demons. It would mean asking Ricard's permission— or worse, his indulgence. But Conner would probably back her up, certainly more than any hunt for the supernatural.

They would go back to the source. And she wasn't thinking of Cranberry Cove for this visit.

FIVE: BEFORE

A bassline thumped from far down the hallway, and Emberly guessed that would be Duke's apartment, one of the three his father had gifted him. She didn't know the others' functions, only that Duke liked to entertain guests here. He hadn't chosen the meeting place, or else they would probably be gathered in one of his father's establishments, but Ricard had told Emberly and Conner where to find his son, and he had told Duke not to go anywhere.

From the sound of the music, loudening at each step, Duke wasn't in the mood to see anyone. In an entertainment space, a makeshift bachelor pad, he could be lost to all manner of substances and distractions.

"How is he?" Emberly asked. "Did Ricard say?"

"Temperamental," Conner warned.

Emberly didn't ask another question. Duke could behave however he needed, if only he would walk them through that day at Cranberry Cove, moment by moment, with all the horror that entailed.

The hallway seemed endless, a sterile tunnel of soft gray carpet and bright blue walls. Duke's door stood at the end, and the bronze doorknob throbbed under Emberly's fingertips to the pounding music's heartbeat. She flashed Conner a questioning look.

He chinned at the door. They wouldn't get anywhere by waiting out in the hall.

Emberly led the way inside and let Conner shut the door. The air pulsed in her ears, against her skull, and she scanned the room in search of the source.

Black amplifiers perched in high corners like vultures gazing down on a corpse. The walls wore a deep red hue, almost cranberry in color. A pillar broke up the center of an open space, though Emberly guessed it acted more as decoration than as a load-bearing structure. Neon lights curled over velvet-coated furniture. A dark patch of tile formed a makeshift dance floor, empty today, and a stained bar haunted one side of the room, its face jutting with barstools, its back lined with shelves full of liquor in clear bottles.

Duke had done everything in his power to carve this space into a nightclub's imitation, but the atmosphere was all wrong. No sweat stink, no crush of bodies, no commotion. Only the face of what this apartment pretended to be and none of the soul.

It almost seemed to welcome Emberly's and Conner's intrusion.

They found Duke with a small glass in one hand

standing at the bar. Ice crackled in a honey-colored brew. He wore a black jacket with yellow warning stripes along the sleeves. Zippers gaped open down his pants like hungry mouths with silver teeth. He was not dressed for business in any way his father would have liked to see.

"Want anything?" he asked without greeting. He'd cut his hair since Emberly last saw him, buzzed close to the scalp. Lines creased his face, and gray flesh pooled beneath his eyes. They twitched from Conner to Emberly and back. "A drink? No? How about a smoke?"

"Trying to quit," Conner said, thumbing to his bicep, where a fresh nicotine patch must have nestled under his jacket.

Duke shrugged, downed his drink, and then poured another.

"How much have you had?" Emberly asked.

Duke didn't answer. Either he couldn't hear her over the thudding music, or he needed all his concentration to fill his glass.

Conner walked the room's edges until he found a small white box on a cluttered end table. His hand ran along its side, and the music shrank to half its volume.

Duke pointed across the room without turning from the bar. "Don't touch that."

"We need to chat," Conner said. "You're not drunk yet. Taken anything else? Anything that might get in the way of us talking this through?"

"I'm not high," Duke said. He carried his glass

from the bar toward a circle of furniture. "I get high to feel things more intensely, and I'm not in the mood for intensity right about now, okay? That enough questions? You two done here?"

Conner raised an open hand. "Take it easy."

"How the fuck am I supposed to take it easy?" Duke thumped onto the couch. "You tell me."

Conner lowered his hand and went quiet.

Duke nodded at him and then at Emberly. "You two stand like cops. Like you're on that *SVU* show. My girl likes us to watch, and this shit is exactly like that shit." He sipped his drink and studied the pair again. "No, I'm not up to talk with you, or you, and definitely not the fucking both of you."

Conner opened his mouth and then shut it. His gaze crawled toward Emberly in unsteady inches, a hope in his expression that she could peel this moment open and find a way through.

She had nothing to offer. What was she supposed to do, argue that Duke should talk with them? Preach how if they didn't sort this out, that would mean letting Ricard go to war over it? Why should he care? Any discussion was a walk on thin glass. To ask about the hotel and Duke's time there would only shatter delicate relations and cut them upon blood-streaked shards.

And he was right; they stood like cops. They were even talking like cops, asking what he was drinking, smoking, ingesting. It wasn't their business. None of this was.

But Emberly couldn't slide back out the door and let the bassline swell to a dragon's heartbeat behind her. Not without answers. She couldn't let Ricard make war if he was in the wrong.

"Duke?" Emberly's heels sank into soft carpet as she approached the circle of furniture. "We aren't going to interrogate you. Your father said you couldn't leave until you talked to us, but we're not the type to push that point."

Duke stared her up and down. "So what then? I ask you to go, and you'll go?"

"Let me you ask you something," Emberly said. "If you think it leads back to Cranberry Cove, we'll keep talking about it. And if it doesn't, then we won't."

"Like what?" Duke said. He probably meant it to sound aggressive, but his words hung tired from his lips.

Emberly swallowed. She needed this to come out exactly right. "I want to know, before you went to Cranberry Cove, did you believe in ghosts?"

Duke blinked at her, sipping his drink.

"And I want to know if that's changed since you left," Emberly said.

She felt Conner's gaze burning into her, but she refused to turn and look at him. She already knew what he thought—what he believed. But this was about Duke's memory, Duke's beliefs, and how they infected and transformed each other. She would watch only him until he answered.

His eyes twitched to her. They were pale and gray, the irises wreathed by thin blood vessels.

He blinked away from her. A heavy sigh shuddered out of him, and his tough guy posture melted into the couch cushions. He was curling against the soft furniture, shrinking into his jacket. A hand jutted over his knees and beckoned for Emberly and Conner to come closer, to sit in the circle of furniture.

Emberly glanced at Conner, but he wouldn't look at her. Wouldn't waste this moment's chance.

They each stepped into the circle, chose a soft seat, and then turned their attention to Duke. Conner sat with his elbows on his thighs, his hands steepled over his lap, his fingers knitting and unknitting. Emberly sat up straight.

Duke faced the floor. "My girl," he said. "She knows something's bothering me, but I can't tell her this shit. And then she gets pissed, like I'm holding out on her. Saying we're disconnected. Not like I don't care about her. What am I supposed to fucking do, talk to her?"

"Couldn't say for sure," Conner muttered. "You don't want relationship advice from the twice divorced."

Duke gestured at Emberly without turning eyes to her again. "What about you? Got any wisdom from your—what's it called? Your woman's intuition?"

Emberly spoke in a slow, gentle tone. "I don't think you're *supposed* to do anything. But if she knows something's wrong, then yes, eventually you might want to talk to her."

She left out any suggestion that his talk with her and Conner might make good practice.

Duke looked from one to the other again. "You won't believe me," he said, a hopeless weight settling on his shoulders. He bent toward a glass coffee table and dug for a cigarette and lighter. "It's not the kind of thing anybody believes."

"We'll do our best," Emberly said. She reached over the coffee table and helped Duke light his cigarette.

A stillness sank its fingers into the room. Emberly sat straight again, but now she needed every inch of self control to keep from shuddering when she looked around.

There was another presence here. Not an entity like she had heard knocking or felt sniffing behind her at Cranberry Cove, but a thoughtless gravity that suggested she should not be encouraging Duke to speak, that she would soon feel the world's axis shift, and nothing would be the same.

Too late to stop it. She had done exactly as Conner hoped, found a method to peel this conversation open, and now Duke was going to talk with them. Whatever fingers held this room, everyone present was in their grasp, and there was no getting out.

"You're with friends here," Conner said, in a smooth, welcoming tone. "It's okay. Tell us what happened."

SIX: AFTER

Half an hour later, Emberly returned to the sterile hallway with Conner close behind her. He shut the door to Duke's apartment, and within seconds the music roared back, too loud for anyone to hear their own thoughts. Exactly as Duke needed.

Emberly pretended not to notice as she started down the hall. Conner either pretended the same, or he was genuinely too uncomfortable to care.

Nothing felt right. Duke's comment again rang through Emberly's mind, that they stood like cops, belonged on TV, and Emberly couldn't blame him. It hadn't turned into an interrogation on their end, but he had answered as if stuffed into a small room with a stiff chair and an uneven table that danced between which three legs it would stand on.

Emberly felt the filth of standing on the other side of that table. The uselessness of it, and the cruelty, too, of encouraging a survivor to parse through a spiderweb of trauma. She liked to think of herself as a professional scalpel, but right now she felt like a careless hammer, the iron head forged into the shape of a hog.

"He didn't see anything," Conner said when they were halfway down the blue hallway. A dismissive note colored his tone, as if he were saying Duke's recounting had been a waste of their time. Almost worthless.

Emberly corrected him. "He didn't see anyone," she said. "That's the same as you and me."

"Doesn't make it a ghost." Conner looked over his shoulder, back at Duke's door. "Or a devil."

No, but it did make a pattern. The snuffling of the guy-thing at Emberly's back, and the *animal* one of those true crime podcast hosts had heard inspecting her in the dark—Duke had heard the same. That recounting of his experience echoed Emberly's and the podcast host's, except he'd faced less hesitation from his attacker. Less assessment needed.

Like it had known Duke was closer to what it was looking for than either podcast host. Than Emberly. *Summoner. Grant. Where?*

"You led him," Conner said.

Emberly snapped to him. "I did no such thing."

"It was a leading question, about ghosts."

"Cut me some slack, Conner. I had to get him talking, and you were out of ideas."

"Right," Conner said. "But it led the whole conversation. I know a thing or two on that, from CPS swinging by when I was a kid, that they have

54

to ask careful questions. People like to have the right answers. You suggest what those answers are, it distorts the info. Taints it."

"It didn't taint anything for me," Emberly said.

She thought again of the true crime podcast. *It came sniffing at me, like it was looking for food*, Stephanie had said to Vivian, except she'd had no idea what her visitor had really been seeking. Neither had Duke. Had he been inventing a story to please Emberly, he wouldn't have known this detail, or he would have come to the same conclusion about it.

The guy-thing hadn't asked Duke a question. It had come to its own conclusion, and then it had hurt him.

"He's making a mistake," Conner said. They were nearing the hall's end, where an elevator waited to take them down four floors. "A few of them."

"You don't believe him?" Emberly asked.

"I wouldn't put it that way exactly." Conner reached the elevator first and pressed the call button. Its burnt-orange eye glowed in the wall. "But it's a trauma defense. Or survival tactic. Makes people forget details, or confuse them into new stories. I know from experience. Had to work on it in counseling, and even now, whole chunks of my childhood are sitting out of order. Even if we talked through every single one, tried to rearrange them back to a truer chronology, I can't promise it would stick. And personally, I'm not all that interested in doing so."

He left unspoken that Duke hadn't been too interested in talking through this one event.

Emberly wondered if the brain jumbling might be the same for her. She couldn't remember whether she had it rough when she was small, could only speculate that was the case by the black chasms in her memory, and she was pretty sure she hadn't spent all those years with the lights off.

And like Conner, it was not an abyss she wanted to challenge in a staring contest. Some things were better left buried.

But not Cranberry Cove.

"He was alone," Emberly said. "He should have stayed alone when Kristof went investigating the sound of someone's knocking. I heard a knocking first, too. And so did Duke, right before hands grabbed his shoulders from behind."

The elevator chimed, and its steely doors slid open, inviting Emberly and Conner into a wood-paneled box. Conner hit the button to the first floor. Another angry eye.

"You say you believe me," Emberly went on. "And you know I wouldn't have talked to Duke before today."

"But he had his back to the other bed and the window," Conner said, sounding annoyed. "Doesn't make sense. There'd have to be hidden paths in the walls, or the floor, somewhere for some creep to slip in and out. That knocking could be a gear grinding while panels slide open."

The elevator hummed as Emberly turned to Conner. "In and out, that quick?"

"Em, what do you want from me?" A haggardness sank into Conner's cheeks, hollowing his big face. "No way we can go to Ricard Morrison and tell him a ghost sexually assaulted his son. We cannot. *I* cannot. He has faith in us, do you know that? Otherwise, he'd have never let us talk to Duke about this."

"I know," Emberly said.

"But that faith will turn dry if we bring him bullshit," Conner said, grinding his teeth between sentences. "Bone dry. We'll be skeletons, all the meat stripped off, worthless at heart. Ricard would never trust our judgment again."

"He would if he couldn't dispute it." The elevator chimed, its doors slid open, and Emberly hurried into a white hallway. "Hell, Conner, I don't know."

"Me neither." Conner walked beside her. His body seemed to throb, as if he carried some of Duke's overloud music in his thick muscles.

They needed answers. The concrete, indisputable kind. Their alternative was letting Ricard wage war on Tyrone and paint the street in blood for no good reason. At this rate, Conner might do something drastic to get this sorted.

Except Emberly couldn't imagine anything too drastic when their investigation so far had come up empty.

"Could go back to the hotel," Conner said. It

sounded like an olive branch. "Try to be ready this time."

In better circumstances, Emberly imagined she would have laughed. Hadn't they been prepared last time? They had carried goddamn semi-automatic shotguns into the time-eaten ruin of Cranberry Cove. If that wasn't ready, she didn't know what readiness looked like.

Conner smirked as if reading her thoughts. "Our guard was down. We thought we were picking through the mess, looking for clues. Our mistake."

"And what would you do differently?" Emberly asked.

"This time, I'll expect a threat," Conner said. "I'll expect a fight."

SEVEN: GHOST

Emberly needed to forget about Cranberry Cove, at least until morning. And force of will alone was not enough to punch that hole in her memory.

When she split from Conner, she swung by her apartment, changed into a black spaghetti-strapped dress, added glittering jewelry she'd never wear on the job, ruby-red earrings of the kind men thought they didn't care about, and a level of makeup that felt like overdoing it, but she made it work. This was the kind of getup that drew the eye and the hand. An outfit to entice the type who would want to distract her and then tear the outfit away.

She avoided greasy dive bars as a rule, but distractions would be easier to find in a forgotten little hellhole with residue from all imaginable narcotics dripping from its every surface. Her intent was to get drunk, fool around, and either go home with someone or take someone home herself.

And likely, she would bring home a mistake. Her

usual. She felt ready to handle dangerous types, knew how to avoid most of them, and for the ones who wouldn't take a hint, she had experience at buying the few seconds she needed to draw out pepper spray or her handgun. Sometimes she missed out on a good thing via misjudged situation. What Duke called *woman's intuition* was a lie to undermine a systemic guessing game based on experience, education, instinct, and a little luck in trying to be less lonely in a carnivorous world. Always vigilant, expecting a moment when she might be overpowered and looking for ways to preempt it. She was used to that.

But the difficult ones were another story. The selfish lovers, the kind who got too attached. That time she went into her bathroom to freshen up and found the guy passed out on her couch.

She would try not to let that last one happen again, at least. The other types, she couldn't really help. She could only do her best and roll the dice.

The alcohol wouldn't take. She could tell from the first sip that her blood had somehow grown an ironclad tolerance of the like unseen in the modern age, and she wouldn't be getting tipsy tonight, let alone drunk. Her thoughts insisted on haunting her body, a physiological manifestation of never letting go.

But she did meet someone.

He was cute enough, the scrawny pale type of near-thirty who wore ragged black clothes and a mop of dark hair and listened to The Cure, his imitation of the outcast Gen-Xer he could never become. Yesteryear would forever dodge his grasp.

Emberly knew the feeling, in an entirely different way, but she wasn't going to think about that tonight, and he was going to help her. He would be the distracting type, the hungry type, the type she could take down if needed.

Except she wasn't going to think about that, either. She was going to bring this guy home, and fuck him, and then drift away in a satisfied haze until dawn brought the world screeching back on sunrays and wakeup alarms.

They had another drink at her apartment. She felt it this time and wondered how much water that dive bar had swirled into their liquor, whether that would ruin their wine—no, the trouble had been her discomfort in a strange place. Here at home, she would quit being trouble and start to have a good time.

She puffed a joint to help her along the path and then settled into making out with her guest. Ricard liked his crew to keep clean, with an exception for his son, but Emberly had long-time experience with this kind of smoke, and she knew sex with strangers went down better with a high.

Her guest's tongue was overeager. He tasted of cheap beer, but she warmed to the flavor as she led him into the bedroom. She ignored his comments about how nice the place was, how beautiful she was, how much he liked the skull and crossbones Jolly

Roger tattoo on her shoulder, peeking out from her dress. None of that mattered. She hadn't invited him here for his assessments.

She showed him better reasons for visiting as they pressed close, slid from each other's clothes, and slipped back onto the bed.

Immediately she noticed a mild tightness. She'd lathered them both from the bottle on her nightstand. What was the trouble? Was she supposed to dilate this afternoon? Did she forget? The high might have made her sensitive, a side effect she'd felt before and should have considered.

"Hang on," she said.

She rolled onto her stomach, tucked her knees underneath her middle, and stretched her arms ahead. There, the position made all the difference. No more discomfort.

Her guest hovered over her from behind. His hands went fumbling along her body, too gentle in some places, too rough elsewhere, but she ignored it. He was doing everything else right, thrusting right, kissing her tattoo.

Until his head leaned past her shoulders. It was only a wet breath behind her head, but the sound seized through her muscles.

Not right now, she thought. She needed to forget about Cranberry Cove.

The high was not the only trouble. Men had told her in the past that she was too sensitive in general.

Skin too thin, hearing too acute. She was doing it again, distracted from her own distraction in a spiral of unpleasant self-sabotage.

Her guest's breath came wet again, a quickness in her ear, weighing upon her. She might not have had enough to drink, but he had gulped down more than was good for him. It made him sloppy, and she wasn't in the mood anymore. She needed to forget Cranberry Cove tonight, but that didn't mean the world would let her.

"Stop," she whispered. And then louder: "Stop."

He stopped, sat back, and then waited, still inside her. She slid from him and turned around again. He looked hurt, an insecure question of *Did I do it wrong?* haunting his puppy eyes, and she briefly wondered if he'd never had the opportunity before.

Pity guided one of her hands to his face, and that remaining need for distraction guided the other. She drew him close, on top of her, her legs bracing his waist. They could try again.

The glee in his eyes was almost pathetic, but he wanted her. She tried to remember a time when that had been enough as he reached over her to grasp the headboard.

His knuckles struck the wood in a clumsy cacophony. Like knocking on a door.

A deflating sigh ran from Emberly's chest, and she shook her head. The momentary thrill was gone, if she had ever found it tonight.

Her guest made a peaceful retreat, said he understood, hurried into his clothes, and left her apartment. She silently wished him a happy masturbation when he got home, or better yet, to meet someone else on the way who would like him better than Emberly did. Someone who wasn't messed up.

But *why* was she messed up? She'd fallen down the hole of a bad trip before, but this high was altogether too gentle. She was entirely present, only a slight tingle in her skin, a brief haze in her head. Weak weed, or a joint decayed. Everything had a shelf life.

Her sensitivity lingered. Not in her body, but in her head. Emberly was the problem, her heart thumping with undesired sensations.

She didn't have a right to these feelings. Nothing had actually happened to her at Cranberry Cove. Only almost happened. Less than that—she'd felt like something almost happened, but even that wasn't true. Nothing was ever going to happen to her there.

She had no right to feel upset, or traumatized, or whatever else was bothering her right now, especially compared to Duke, or the others, or the missing. No right to anything. Because nothing happened to her at Cranberry Cove and nothing would. She was safe.

"Nothing happened," she whispered. "Grow up."

But what about other nights? Other locations? She had known threats before, dealt with them when she could, dodged them when she couldn't. Vigilant in necessary ways, but eventually fortune's dice rolls might glare at her with snake eyes. Threats and encounters nudged the black depths of memory. The empty spaces inside her, ripe for haunting.

She sat in her silk robe at the bed's edge for the longest time, the night crawling over her while she forced her head to keep void of thought. Her pathetic high slipped into weariness.

Part of her had to be waiting for something. A sign. A sound. Validation in ruining her own evening, haunted by what had happened to other people. To herself, in the past. Were such ghosts normal? She had spent so much time concerned for her own safety, rolling her eyes at the carelessness of men like Duke and Conner and the stranger she'd briefly invited into her bed, that the true frailty beneath their bravado only seemed real when she had to listen about and understand they were as mortal as Emberly or anyone else.

Every human being acted invincible in their own way. It was always a lie. They could be taken apart by merciless bacteria, ferocious weather, and each other. Flimsy skeletons bound in tissue, given enough hubris to believe they were special.

When really, they could destroy themselves from the inside. A thought could be a virus, and a memory could melt a soul like hungry acid through flesh.

Even a sound could do it. Snuffling in the ear. A *knock-knock-knock* at the door.

"Nothing happened!" she snapped, louder than she

meant, like someone had cranked up the volume of her internal radio without asking permission first.

It made her jolt off the bed, and she began to pace her apartment. Out of the bedroom, around the living room and kitchen, switching on lights and chasing away shadows. The walls learned to dance when you lived by yourself, and every sound could become a threat. She shouldn't be alone tonight.

And she couldn't stop her thoughts from drifting toward Cranberry Cove.

She tried to focus on the host from *Cold Case Journeys*, laughing off the sounds of what she believed to be an animal inspecting her in the night, but that only made Emberly think of a bear in the woods. Even a curious animal could be a threat. Could hurt you.

But the podcast hosts had turned on their lantern and seen nothing. No raccoon, no dog, no bear. They hadn't seen anyone.

Neither had Duke. He had understood what happened to him, but not the identity or the method. As if someone had crept from the hotel's very surfaces and then melted into them. Small wonder he would now entertain the possibility of ghosts.

At some point in her pacing, Emberly snatched up her phone. Her thumb hovered over the keypad, but she felt the search engine rejecting her, like the internet had something caught in its throat.

Or were her nerves the problem?

The simplicity of it threatened to break the

worlds of pragmatic minds, but she'd always had a sliver of superstition tucked inside her, in the way that checking your horoscope could be meaningless fun until you gave it serious consideration. Someone could shrug off questions of ghosts, or entertain the humor of possibility. To give the supernatural any serious weight meant having to reevaluate the shape of the world.

"What are you afraid of?" Emberly asked herself. "That you're wrong? Or that you're right?"

She was near enough convinced, but Conner wasn't. His words rang through her head. *I don't believe in the boogeyman, or the devil, none of that shit.*

But he believed in Emberly. And what if she believed in the boogeyman? The devil? Worse things? Could Conner twist his denial into a pretzel of believing that she believed yet not believing in what she believed? It was the same infuriating tunnel vision she'd watched in Duke when they first stepped into the nightclub-looking apartment with him, the same empty perspective as Conner at Shipley's Pub, expecting he'd win any fight he rambled his way into.

They could believe in the power of themselves, but that didn't mean the world would give a shit. It would break its own rules to show them differently.

Emberly thought of the old Stephen Crane poem.

> *A man said to the universe:*
> *"Sir, I exist!"*

"However," replied the universe,
"The fact has not created in me
A sense of obligation."

Heart thudding in frustration, molars grinding—she had the sense that long-dead poet had held too kind an outlook for the cosmos. More likely, the universe would reply, *I will drown you in misery. I will dredge up every wonder you can conceive, and I will corrupt it into nightmare. And by the time I am finished, mankind, you will wish you did not exist.*

"Fuck it," Emberly muttered.

She unlocked her phone and typed in what she'd been avoiding since that conversation at Shipley's, since the guy-thing first touched her in that rotted-out hotel.

Cranberry Cove ghost.

Only one new item popped into her immediate search. *These Houses Weep: Real-Life Ghost Hunters* was a streaming channel where two young men ventured into abandoned or supposedly haunted locations to catch evidence of the supernatural. A glance through their page showed numerous hours-long videos cataloging their visits to deserted prisons, closed-down asylums, and active hotels with haunted rooms.

Emberly found nothing of Cranberry Cove until she watched their recent preview videos, short snippets building toward the full streaming event. One ghost hunter wore an orange ballcap backward and a yellow hoodie, his eyes bright. The other flashed a big grin within his goatee, their expressions beaming from the channel's banner. Those same faces appeared in a video from about a year ago, when they had obtained an official permit to film at Cranberry Cove, something those true crime podcast hosts never mentioned in their preparations for sleeping at the hotel. They must have figured no one would care.

Another video showed the ghost hunters—two goofy white guys with a plan and a dream—packing their van with gear. And then another video showed the hotel's grim front at the corner of Washington and Mayhew, with a soundtrack of hollering and joy as the ghost hunter duo set out on another adventure.

That was their last video. No complete hours-long stream, no post-visit tidbits, no highlight reel. Their online channel lay as abandoned as Cranberry Cove itself.

Maybe they'd stepped inside, sensed the danger, and changed their minds. Or, out of some hesitation or respect, the ghost hunters had chosen not to pry any further.

A presence might have scared them out of making their videos entirely. To play with aesthetically creepy yet harmless places had to offer a world of difference from a genuine haunt, and the two men might have found themselves longing for innocence in a world that hated the innocent. Maybe tombs had grown inside them, and the laughter had slid from their faces, and they'd chosen to lead different lives.

Or, they might have disappeared entirely.

There was evil in that hotel. Emberly had never believed in simplistic morality any more than simplistic gender, but she couldn't assume a simple mistake when there seemed to be a devil in the walls.

If only there could be one more *These Houses Weep* video to explain everything. But then, if the internet could give every answer easily, it would know where to find those who had disappeared, too. It would carry lost memories, dead dreams, everything you could ever want.

Emberly didn't expect that sort of digital miracle. There was only more work to do.

She tried new searches. *Cranberry Cove Summoner Grant. Cranberry Cove devil. Cranberry Cove satanism. Cranberry Cove prince of darkness.* The last made her think of Conner's longtime nickname for Duke.

And it brought an unexpected result—the Princes of Darkness, Archives, with the words Cranberry Cove highlighted next to the year 1976.

Emberly tapped her thumb against the screen and scrolled.

The Princes of Darkness were a longstanding club, gathering the eclectic interests of leather aficionados, BDSM practitioners, and Crowleyesque magicians. Founded in 1954, they seemed a sanctuary where local weirdos of all stripes could band together against a society steeped in McCarthyism, absolutism, and other authoritarian nonsense.

Little information popped up on their particular 1976 gathering at Cranberry Cove. A determined member of the organization must have taken to cataloging their meetings and events going back to 1969, probably transcribed from old ledgers and flyers to the website, which looked to have climbed from the primordial digital muck of 1999 at best. During their 1976 convention at Cranberry Cove, the Princes of Darkness had chosen their princess of the year, that being one Angelica Glade. No photos, no further information. Only that moment.

And that name.

The lead was scant. Emberly didn't know Summoner Grant's last name. It could be Glade. The Princes of Darkness and their convention might have seemed unrelated to a careless eye. Most anyone would believe the '70s Cranberry Cove assailant to be a flesh-and-blood man who would age and weaken and die, not a devil or boogeyman or guy-thing.

Emberly couldn't blame them. She might have carried a sliver of superstition, but she'd never full-on believed in magic, occultists, or weird shit before.

But the time period was a match for convention year and the downfall of Cranberry Cove. What else was there to go on?

Emberly bookmarked the page and did a cursory search for locals named Angelica Glade. She needed to latch onto something, be it chasing the ghost hunters, or interviewing the podcasters, or seeking out this now-elderly woman, assuming she was still alive. Emberly's imagination would go wild otherwise, snatching every outlandish possibility.

Her screen again filled with the ghost hunters' faces as she closed a tab covering their derelict streaming channel. She wondered about their smiles and tried not to plant her first gory vision of the hotel upon them. Damn this imagination. She needed another drink to dull it and made for the fridge to get one.

But possibilities kept teasing her anyway. How many people without podcasts or streaming channels, the kind with no desire for fame, had visited Cranberry Cove on a dare, or a joke, or anything? How many had simply wanted a place to sleep for the night? Had they met a guy-thing there and kept their mouths shut?

And how many had no choice but silence because they'd vanished from this world?

There would be no sign of them in streets, homes, or Emberly's search bar. Their absences were a negative she couldn't prove or grasp. The modern world too quickly assumed everything could be found online. Much of the past remained lost, either undocumented or undigitized, from missing persons to their personalities to all evidence they had ever lived. They were relics of fading memories, and by poor luck alone did anyone stumble upon crevices of the bone-and-earth world where you might uncover horrors forever unknown to Siri and Google.

There were more things in Heaven, Earth, and Cranberry Cove than dreamed of in men's philosophy.

And none of them were good or right.

EIGHT: THE HOUSE

Angelica Glade lived on the south side, practically at town's edge. Chest-high weeds coated much of her property, breathing a cloud of gnats where the overgrowth groped at her porch's lattice edges and either side of the driveway.

Gravel crunched beneath Emberly's tires as she parked her little violet Chrysler beside an aged Volkswagen. She picked her way across a lumpy path of flat stones toward the disheveled wooden porch steps. The sun had bleached most of the house's sky-blue paint over the years, leaving only patches of its once-rich color.

A screen door screeched open as Emberly neared the stoop. It swayed against a white scarecrow of a woman who leaned out the front door in a crimson robe three sizes too big for her. She had to be in her seventies, maybe older. Her every feature was a sharp point.

"You're the one who called an hour ago, right?" she asked with a pinched accent. She might have come from Maine, or maybe somewhere in northern Massachusetts. "I'm Angelica Glade. You got to be Emmy, right? That's you?"

"That's me," Emberly said.

She dressed in a more form-fitting jacket and skirt today, the kind Angelica might presume belonged to a secretary or an overachieving grad student. A bulky leather bag hung at her side from a cross-chest strap. She didn't expect to need anything that she kept within, but she would hate for this summer morning to prove her wrong, only to have left her gear in the car.

"Inside then," Angelica said, waving her hand at either Emberly or the gnats. "It'll be too hot out here before long."

The indoors weren't much better. Emberly doubted Angelica had the resources for a decent AC window unit, let alone central air. Through the sweltering foyer, Angelica led toward a living room, where a fan spun lazy circles from the ceiling.

Had coming here been the right idea? Emberly might have found better luck searching for those wayward ghost hunters or contacting the true crime podcasters to see what they'd left out of their Cranberry Cove episode. Maybe she should have chased an errant detail Duke had mentioned, if she could think of one. Angelica Glade was local, but that didn't make her the best lead.

"Make yourself comfy," Angelica said, gesturing

at the living room. "I'm not prone to visitors much these days, except the mailman. Or mailwoman. They change it so much, it's a wonder I even get my junk mail."

She disappeared around a corner. Porcelain clacked out of sight, where she might be readying coffee cups or a plate of cheese and crackers.

Emberly wasn't sure how to make herself comfortable. She could only be grateful this line of work had put her in far worse situations, and often not of her own doing.

The living room was the confused offspring of a garage sale, a new age shop, and the props department for some low-budget Satanic horror movie. Dishes of brass and tin formed towers to one side, glinting with the window-cast sunshine of early morning. Lit candlesticks drooled creamy wax along end tables, shelves, and a desk crowded with old magazines, liable to catch fire if even one candle were knocked over. The pages looked to be a mix of ancient grocery store checkout aisle tabloids and the kind you might find moldering in a sex shop twenty years ago. Pentacles mingled with pentagrams over the yellowing wallpaper. Crucifixes joined them in some places, alongside symbols Emberly couldn't identify. There were cardboard boxes too, some shut by their fellows stacked on top, others overflowing with papers, clothing scraps, baubles on thin chains, and in one place a belt glittering with rhinestones.

It was too much for Emberly to take in, and the bulk of it squeezed around her. Only the presence of an oven, fridge, and faucet to one side suggested a separation between living room and kitchen, but otherwise the junk pile stretched throughout the house.

The mess carried on toward a dark hallway at the living room's back end. If a basement lurked beneath the house, Emberly expected the mess lurked there too, first on steel shelves, and then coating the floor in detritus.

Most homeowners would apologize for this kind of junkyard, but Angelica seemed too old to give a damn. With any luck, Emberly wouldn't have to worry about it either. She had come to Angelica's house for information, not to dissect her hoard.

But the house didn't feel like a hoarder's nest. Emberly had stepped inside one of those before, during a collection for Ricard, and the atmosphere had carried obsessive disarray and a lack of control.

Angelica's house had a compact nature, like a fist tightened around a treasured jewel. Its warmth came less from sunshine and poor airflow, more from the oppressive heat of those grasping fingers, desperate to hold its possessions and never let them go, even if it had to crush them into place.

A tightness sucked at Emberly's throat. She rubbed beneath her sweat-dotted jaw, past a faded scar, dropping her fingers to her clavicle as if stroking a piece of unchewed meat down her esophagus. She almost wanted to ask Angelica for a glass of water, but she doubted this discomfort had anything to do with her insides.

It was the house. And something *in* the house. At Duke's apartment, the weight of the moment had intruded on their conversation. Here, there was an unconscious force imposing on Emberly's presence. She was not wanted. Angelica could invite her in, but that did not mean she should stay.

If Cranberry Cove truly held a ghost, and so the supernatural was real, then this place, too, was haunted.

This was the right line of inquiry to chase. Even if this house couldn't answer Emberly's every question, there was a connection. She could feel it in the air. The smell of it exhaled from the smoke-scented furniture.

Emberly stepped around a crate of wrinkled tapestries, shoved a cardboard box of jangling trinkets aside, and made room for herself on a tattered beige couch. A circular glass table stood ahead. It held an incense burner at its center, the underside choked with brick-colored ashes. Papers surrounded it, their faces marked by strange symbols in black and red ink.

On the far side of the table stood a gargantuan burgundy chair, its fabric patched over with scraps, even denim in one place. It was too large for Angelica's tiny frame. Emberly guessed it came with the house, same as Angelica's robe.

Or both were meant for someone else.

Angelica appeared beside the couch and hurried to clear away papers. She laid two wooden coasters in their place. Her hands looked pristine for her age, unworn by wrinkles, olive spots, or a leathery texture. The nails were white and sharp.

"You'll want coffee, yes?" Angelica asked, though it didn't sound like a question. "Cream, sugar? Not sure I have such things, but I'm up, so I'm willing to hunt them down."

"Black is fine," Emberly said. She should sound cheerful, put on airs of gratitude for this meeting, but the sweat sliding down her spine set a chill in her skin. "Thank you."

Angelica gave a firm nod and disappeared into the kitchen again. "I'm sorry I could only give you options of early morning or late evening when you called at dawn." Cabinets banged beneath her wandering hands. Something crinkly spilled onto a metal dish. "I sleep much of the day, and the night too. I'm a twilight sort, always have been."

"That's fine, Mrs. Glade." Emberly gazed over the cluttered treasures. "I appreciate your making time to see me."

"Mrs. Glade," Angelica scoffed. "Call me miss, please. Or Angelica, that'll do us better. I detest marriage. I don't believe in it."

Emberly doubted that meant Angelica disbelieved in companionship, considering that hint she'd found on the Princes of Darkness website. Angelica might live alone here, but she hadn't always. Or she kept mementos of the past.

Or she didn't live alone. Time would tell.

Emberly hugged her bag close and dug her fingertips into its side, where the leather creased around the reassuring shape of her handgun. She didn't expect to need it.

But better to have it here in case this morning proved her wrong.

NINE: SUPERSTITION

Dawn's light painted a welcoming scarlet beauty across the sky as Conner parked his Mazda at one corner of Washington and Mayhew, and none of that splendor passed to Cranberry Cove. The building remained the gray tumbledown he had seen the other day. It had lingered in this state for decades, and it would keep on lingering that way until it finally collapsed, haunted and unloved.

Haunted. The word rankled Conner as he killed the engine and eased his seat back a few inches. He might be sitting here for a while, waiting for the results of calling in a favor yesterday evening. Better he get comfortable until he had to force himself onto his feet and into that stale crypt. This early in the summer day, he could get away with merely cracking a window over running the car's AC.

Shadows stalked the cracked sidewalk of Washington Avenue. Street kids were the true ghosts of this town, fading and forgotten. Vampires might slink through the alleyways.

"Enough creatures of the night," Conner said, switching on the radio to an oldies station.

He had kept himself mostly sober last night, sipping only a quick whiskey to help get him to bed. Hopefully that wasn't the case for Emberly. Between the Cranberry Cove encounter the other day, Ricard's follow-up chastisement, and yesterday's painful conversation with Duke, Emberly had plenty of reason to drink deep, smoke herself silly, and forget her last visit to this cursed place.

Not that she would actually forget. Often she remembered too much for her own good. Even if she couldn't recall a particular unsavory memory, her body had written the past into her muscles and nerves. Conner saw it whenever a situation dared glance at going sideways.

Ricard knew it, too. That was likely why he wanted Emberly to keep her distance from Cranberry Cove.

In a way, they were all being ridiculous. Conner's mother had been the same. She once bought a black goat from a farm upstate, with intentions of sacrificing it in some occult ceremony to protect the family at the next full moon. Conner had slipped the rope from its neck and chased it out of the back yard. Never found out what became of it, but he couldn't let his mother slit its throat over nonsense, even if she slapped him, even if she told his father, with all the worse consequences that would have entailed.

Conner's father never heard about the goat when he came back from his most recent trucking job. His mother didn't punish Conner in that instance, either. She interpreted the animal's mysterious absence as a sign of household blessing and never mentioned it again.

So sure, Conner understood Emberly's entertaining the supernatural. That was an ordinary woman thing, and for all her extraordinary traits, she was as much a devotee to astrological hangups, ghostly presences, and generalized magical thinking as any other girl.

But Ricard—he knew better. He had to be looking out for Emberly's own good, humoring her, same as Conner.

And then there was Duke. He must have known better, same as his father, until Emberly dragged the word *ghost* into their meeting yesterday. She may have succeeded in breaking the ice, but it hadn't done any good for their investigation, let alone Duke's wellbeing.

Conner would have to fix it all. Nothing new there. Grit his teeth, get his hands dirty, prove there was nothing more to Cranberry Cove than an old building, its solid-world secrets, and a sick man who needed to be put down like a rabid dog.

Emberly would call Conner's approach insulting, disrespectful, sexist—a million words he'd forget in a day or so in the shadow of caring about her. Such names meant nothing when they were true. Those eyes saw right through him, and he didn't mind.

Deep down, he wanted Emberly out of this business. Any debt she owed Ricard in treatments and reshaped flesh, Conner would shoulder it.

Really, she would be doing him a favor. He would worry less.

An hour crawled by while he listened to the oldies station dance between '70s and '80s hits and awaited an important phone call. Evidence of a favor repaid.

General knowledge and childhood common sense told him any boogeyman worth his closet would skitter off from decent lighting. Even a kid's nightlight would do. A ridiculous perspective, but there was real-world application for it. Those same bright bulbs would reveal signs of trapdoors and secret passages, and then Conner would prove that whoever had attacked Emberly, and maybe Duke, had been nothing more ethereal than flesh and blood.

And Conner would spill that blood.

Sunlight warmed the street but refused to give it any color, only harshening one shade of gray over another. Had local businesses and residences sent this patch of town crumbling by mutual agreement? Or had Cranberry Cove's downfall spread to everything it could see and touch? Even the sun had little business gracing the abandoned hotel.

Conner's phone hummed beside the stick shift. That would be Latoya, and the favor. He dragged the phone to his ear without a word.

"You're in business," Latoya said in dry whisper.

"But we're even now, Bohme. Also, if you flip a light switch and it all goes up in smoke? Don't blame me. Those wires have been mouse food since God-knows-when."

"Since the '70s." Conner smirked against his phone. "You're an angel, Latoya."

"Yeah, yeah, let there be light." Latoya wished him good luck and hung up.

"God-knows-when," Conner muttered to himself.

He shoved open the driver's door and slammed it shut with his eyes on the hotel, as if daring it to respond. It stood silent, unmoving.

Conner scoffed. "That's what I thought."

He ambled to the Mazda's trunk and fetched his black shotgun, loaded with every expectation for blowing holes through rotted plaster walls. And maybe floors, and the ceiling, too. He had come to fight an unseen enemy, and had he stayed on the phone a moment longer with Latoya, he could've promised her there were no mice chewing up the wires in Cranberry Cove.

Rodents knew better than to cross this threshold. Only men were so foolish as to believe they owned the world.

Conner crossed the street, pawed through the dark lobby, and found wall switches beside the dusty check-in desk. Lightbulbs flickered alive across dangling electric chandeliers. Water damage might have warped the ceiling, but the wires held strong for now, and Conner planned to make a swift exit if he smelled smoke.

Doubtful that Emberly would be awake this early in the day, at least after the night she should have given herself as a treat. Conner slipped out his phone and shot her a quick text anyway. She would find it when she finally woke up. Kindness dictated he let her know he'd arrived, and he would check in now and then. She would worry otherwise.

Completely unnecessary. He could take care of himself. As far as he was concerned, worrying was his job between the two of them. Ricard had made the right call in taking Emberly off this matter. Conner certainly didn't want her checking out Cranberry Cove again.

If the longevity of electrical infrastructure seemed unnatural, he wouldn't think on it too hard. Emberly might say not thinking too hard was his specialty. Do first, think second.

He crept toward the main stairway, shotgun braced to his chest, and eyed the shadowy patch at the landing between floors. Two days ago, the same darkness had driven an icicle down his spine. He hadn't said a word about it to Emberly, but the landing here seemed ghostlier than anything else, its fingers threatening to reach for him.

Ridiculous. All of it. His fingers could threaten too, easy as flipping a wall switch.

Another set of bulbs flared to life, and their light

stripped the shadowy patch clean off the stairway. It became what it had always been—an ordinary landing, its carpet scuffed through to wooden flooring, the nearby wallpaper having faded and peeled with time.

But there was no ghost to this spot. No supernatural maw to devour those who stepped here. Only the brief pause between one set of steps and another, up to the second floor of Cranberry Cove.

"Let there be light," Conner said, planting a shoe at the foot of the stairway. "And let the devil fear it."

TEN: PRINCESS

A quake unsettled Emberly's bag. She snapped it open and dug gently past her handgun, where her phone had slid between a pad of tissues and a compact mirror. It glowed with a text message.

CONNER: Got CC bright like a Christmas tree

Emberly held her breath not to groan. Conner thought he was playing the hero, banishing the darkness. Would he have the wariness to keep safe in a place like Cranberry Cove? After a couple minutes, she hurried out a reply before Angelica could return from the kitchen with her coffee.

EMBERLY: be careful

CONNER: Always, and you too

EMBERLY: yes I know you care

CONNER: With all the grace of a brick, but it's honest

Emberly wanted to keep talking, but she would only distract him. He'd bent his thoughts too far toward her protection, and that meant keeping subtle walls between them.

She could trust him to care, but not always to help. Each time a bad moment came her way, she had to seal it tight behind her lips. A skull made a good cage for secrets, and Conner was too much of a boy and a knight even in his early forties for Emberly to share with him about that evening two months back when a handsy man outside Shipley's Pub wouldn't take no for an answer. Delicious as breaking one of his fingers had felt, his mewling cries never stripped the memory of his touch from Emberly's skin.

It lingered, even now.

And she couldn't share incidents before that with Conner, either. The young man at that New Year's party who thought she hadn't noticed him drop a tablet into her red plastic cup. And the drunk who'd groped between Emberly's legs a year before her surgery. And the curious dockhand who'd spotted the edge of her Jolly Roger shoulder tattoo and wanted to see the rest without asking.

All those who felt entitled to touch or speak to her, who noticed her early in her transition and chose to make her life a living hell, who demanded she be grateful for their attention. Each time she stepped out into the world, there was a chance of threat. A roll of the dice.

Conner didn't understand. He saw these types of incidents as flareups in the flesh of civilization, not a constant everyday persistence. As existence.

What was Emberly supposed to say? *Call it a symptom of the pink tax?* She would sound like she was talking nonsense.

Conner couldn't know her general experiences or any singular experience, from traumatic monument to typical street harassment, when anything he said or did was useless against both past and future. Nothing had ever happened, far as he knew, even when something had. To share would only burden him with rage. Kind as he might be toward Emberly, he wouldn't be kind to himself for his failure to travel through time and undo these moments. Perhaps he never thought of being overpowered in body, but his soul knew better.

Easier to be silent, no matter how much he cared for her.

"Cranberry Cove," Angelica called from the kitchen. Her voice grew louder with each word, a warning of her approach. "That's what you were calling about. You're lucky I keep the hours I do."

"I know," Emberly said. "I'm grateful."

"Well, mine's not quite a busy schedule these days." Angelica stepped into the living room carrying two scratched-up coffee mugs, both black. One bore a painted skull and crossbones, an echo of Emberly's ink.

"It's for a paper." Emberly thanked Angelica again and took the coffee she would only pretend to sip. This was not a household she could trust. "One I've been putting off, and firsthand sources are the best kind."

"That was a long time ago," Angelica said, circling the coffee table. "Only went there once, you know."

"I did not," Emberly said.

Angelica eased into her oversized burgundy seat, and the giant robe folded around her. She looked almost childlike sitting between the chair's massive arms, a shrunken figure against its gargantuan back. Her tiny shape clutched the steaming mug as if she'd come in moments ago from playing in the snow and needed hot cocoa with marshmallows.

"The Princes of Darkness," Angelica said, almost nostalgic. "Those were the days. We were outsiders everywhere we went, but hell, they made me feel queenly. You should've seen me, I was quite the prize."

"Do you have photos?" Emberly asked.

"Never, never." Angelica waved a hand through coffee steam. "Back then, we kept our business quiet. No pictures, that was a rule. I could never understand when the queerer bunch of us would pose for snapshots outside our club gatherings, like they thought if they meant well, the photos wouldn't get slurped up by some homophobic fuck with a dark room."

Emberly blew across the rim of her mug. "I understand."

She meant it, too. She'd spoken with her elders, people of a different time, and people who'd come into themselves in the '80s, before digital made capturing every moment a breeze. Photographs weren't easy like these days. Film was expensive then, and few had a Polaroid or dark room to handle development.

And monetary cost aside, there were dangers to evidence. Queer folk back then had to keep long memories when photographs could fall into the wrong hands and shatter lives.

"I don't expect you to remember everything about Cranberry Cove," Emberly said.

Angelica sipped her coffee and aimed the mug across the table. "Well, you should. I'll never forget that night. Hard to shake the moment you met the man of your heart."

Emberly held herself still as she glanced over the tremendous chair, the occult decorations, and the robe draping Angelica's rail-thin body. She had guessed right. Angelica might not believe in marriage, but she did not live in this packed little house by herself. There was a giant here, perhaps bigger than Conner, someone fit to make a throne of that enormous burgundy chair.

"I've had a lot of loves," Angelica went on. "Before him, alongside him. What would you kids call it today? I don't know, but that was us. We were free lovers, and the Princes of Darkness—well, in togetherness, we were safe. That autumn of '76, the club rented out Cranberry Cove's convention hall and dining area. We didn't tell them what for, of course, but they could've figured it out with enough rubbing the old brain cells together. Princes of Darkness. What did they think we were, Black Sabbath wannabes? Didn't matter. It was a private engagement, otherwise they'd have called the cops. You know how it is."

Emberly gave a slow nod.

"Anyway, the club named me princess that night." Angelica laughed into her coffee, sending brown droplets bouncing. "Meant nothing in the long-term way, purely ceremonial. Got to have your fun, right? And we had our fun all the time, giving each other titles, desecrating the memory of monarchies in our own manner. We did that all the time. No power to it besides choosing a partner, and anyone could refuse. Of course, my refusal was the issue. There was a man that night—Hob, or Bob—funny, I don't know for sure? Bodybuilder sort, a real cock of the walk, you know?"

"I try not to," Emberly said, one hand squeezing her knee. "But yes, I've known the type."

"Of course, he wanted me to choose him," Angelica said, leaning back. "Damn, did he. The princess and her lackey. He was persistent, insistent. Really made him sore when I passed up his wall of muscle for my sweet sorcerer."

Emberly's nails dragged over her thigh. The tension stiffened her arms and back, but she couldn't see a reason for it, only felt it bone-deep. Woman's intuition, as Duke would call it, and he'd be wrong. More like someone walking on her grave.

Or maybe it was the fabric of the universe rubbing

against her body like a snake shedding its skin against a rock. She might feel the friction, but the presence would slither away, leaving only the translucent warning that a larger, more dangerous universe than the one she used to know now hunted existence. A universe where the impossible was true.

"Sorcerer," Emberly echoed. She watched Angelica take another sip of coffee, her mind clearly wading into an ocean of nostalgia.

"Oh, it'll sound like nonsense to your generation, I'm sure." Angelica let out a pleasant sigh. "But back then, we knew. In the secret places, you could keep a wild world alive. Our time was over by the next decade, despite all those silly idiots caterwauling about Satan and board games and heavy metal in the '80s. But for a span, those princes of mine knew true darkness. My heart knew it best."

"Your heart." Emberly felt hers thudding.

"Yeah," Angelica said, wistful. "My love, Grant Lodestar."

Ice crackled down Emberly's spine with a wintry bite and glacial weight, as if a cold breastbone now pressed against her back. She leaned forward without meaning to, fighting her own body and its muscle memory.

She could imagine a snuffling creature might soon touch her hair and skin, moments before asking its awkward question in a vicious whisper.

Summoner. Grant. Where?

ELEVEN: METHOD

Conner hummed to himself as he paced Room 2A for the dozenth time. The song's name and lyrics eluded him, risen from the past, heard second on the radio this morning, but since then an hour's worth of other songs and nervous tension had buried everything besides the tune. That didn't keep him from humming it, but the forgetfulness added another layer to his frustration beneath the unyielding glow of the ceiling light.

The summer day had rolled in fast since he stepped into the hotel. Its stale air baked the stuffy upstairs, and Conner quickly worked up a sweat as he walked the room and tested the furniture. He slid the nightstand to one corner, dragged the dresser from the wall, and shoved the twin beds together at the room's center, clearing 2A's perimeter. One open palm stroked every surface—the walls, the electric fixtures, the dresser and nightstands. He moved both beds around to fully inspect the floor.

Soft plaster and filthy carpet alike held firm beneath

his fingers. He slit the carpet open with a boxcutter and peeled it back from the hard floor, looking for panels, hinges, but there was nothing to indicate secret passages under or between rooms.

Like Emberly's assailant had come from nowhere and returned there.

"That makes no fucking sense," Conner told the room.

He switched from stroking the walls to knocking on them, first with his fist, and then with the butt of his shotgun. The plaster caved into valleys in some places. Elsewhere he beat dark holes into the walls, but no curious eyes peered from the blackness. Not even animal stares.

Conner thought of serial killer houses, of plastic-wrapped skeletons hidden within wiring and insulation, their sockets glaring out through dust and time.

There were disappearances, too, Emberly had said.

Conner had no choice but to believe her. He had little knack for internet research and no patience for parsing through newspaper clippings. He worked best in the world of firm surfaces, vague scents, and an instinct for the right and wrong of a situation.

Cranberry Cove could only distort his notions for so long before he cracked it apart.

He left Room 2A and returned to the stairs, making a hurried climb to the third floor, and then the fourth, checking down their hallways for unlocked doors.

Not one doorknob yielded to his touch. He expected the same elsewhere, and he wasn't going to kill his back and thighs running up to the fifth, sixth, and seventh floors to find no entry.

Cranberry Cove was shut up tight. There might be bodies hidden in these rooms, but without digging downstairs for keys, he had no way to know.

And he doubted it mattered. Room 2A was the site of Duke's attack and Emberly's encounter. Even if Conner broke open one of these other rooms and found a secret passage to Room 2A, he should have been able to find the reverse route from within.

He was humming again as he stormed back down to the second floor. The notes came forced through his lips in frustrated bursts. Likely the original song was not an angry one, but this was his rendition, the only kind he knew when he couldn't remember the lyrics, the name, everything clinging to the edges of his mind in the same way an explanation for Cranberry Cove haunted the edges of reality.

This place hid a mysterious intruder whose route seemed ghostlike and untraceable. It wasn't right. Conner should have found something by now.

"How'd you do it?" he muttered. "How do you get in and out, you bastard?"

There had to be a method someone could tear apart or replicate. Something Kristof had missed, or a detail that Duke had lost in his traumatized confusion. Conner didn't blame him. He used to remember picking savage fights in Penbrook Park, the giant teen boy thundering his fists into other teens' faces and guts, leaving a trail of shiners, bloody noses, and cracked ribs. Only through counseling had he pieced together that these were moments of retaliation. That he hadn't always been an adolescent giant, but a small creature with vengeance growing in his guts until it blossomed in later years.

He was going to find vengeance now, stepping again into Room 2A, his shotgun ready for a figure to leap from the shadows. His humming turned shaky.

Trauma only explained Duke's experience. Conner was stronger than most, but he also trusted Emberly's judgment. And his own eyes and ears. No one had come scuttling out of this room and into the second-floor hallway two days ago.

If anyone had been here, they had another escape route.

Conner paced along the walls again, digging his hands into the rotted insulation and unchewed wiring. These hands would flip the beds, tear away the dresser, unmake the bathroom. Somehow, in some way, Room 2A would give up its secrets. Conner would uncover the ladder to a Prohibition-era distillery, or the passages that turn-of-last-century innkeepers used to rob wealthy guests, or bits of body parts thrown down chutes in an ode to Chicago's murder castle of old.

No matter how ludicrous, Cranberry Cove would

offer him a rational answer. It would tell him where to find the guy-thing who dared put hands on Emberly.

TWELVE: SEX MAGIC

Emberly sank so deeply into her thoughts that she almost sipped the coffee before remembering not to trust the drink, not even from this harmless-looking older woman in her gray hair and giant robe.

A robe which likely belonged to a man named Grant. Same with the gargantuan chair where Angelica sat.

Emberly cleared her throat and forced herself to speak. "You called Grant a sorcerer?" she asked. "That's an unusual word for someone. And you met him at Cranberry Cove?"

"Only reason I remember it," Angelica said. Her eyes misted with memory. "Though that night, I couldn't have known he'd become my heart. Nobody ever plans these changes of self. One minute, you're out to have a good time, not a long time, no thoughts for the future, only the spark of right now. Men are plentiful, you chew through them like bubblegum."

Emberly's failed date flitted through her mind. She gave a stern nod.

Angelica nodded back as her lips spread in a knowing smile. "But then there'll be an evening, and a certain man, and you'll feel the safety of his arms and decide you want this forever. It'll burst like fireworks inside you. And you'll never forget the place, the night, the moment. Even when it feels like no big deal at the time, if it matters later, the source is apt to stick. I get it, we women are supposed to be independent and the like these days, but honestly, sometimes it feels good to be rescued."

Emberly kissed the coffee mug's lip and thought of Conner's concern. Had he returned to the hotel today for Ricard, or did he mean to protect Emberly from whatever lurked in Cranberry Cove?

Such a boy for a man in his age. Such a knight for a man of Ricard's crew.

"But you want to know about that evening," Angelica went on, dragging Emberly's attention back across the coffee table. "Cranberry Cove, 1976."

Emberly set down her mug. "I do. For the paper."

"Grant was never much for academia." Angelica took another sip of coffee and set down her mug, too. "More about the application of his arts. He had a few years on me. I was a nubile thing, and the gray had kissed his temples already." She smoothed her hair over one ear. "But he was a big, soft man, like a guardian bear, and he dabbled in every domain held dear by the Princes of Darkness. The leather, the domination."

"The occult magic," Emberly said.

"Sex magic." Angelica laughed, big and open-mouthed, setting a candlelit gleam across her teeth. "Better than a vibrator, you know? Better than dreams."

Emberly glanced to her bag, where her phone again lay hidden beside her handgun. Should she pretend to take notes, or would that distract Angelica? More than anything, Emberly wanted to search *Cranberry Cove sex magic*.

But a firsthand source sat across from her. Whatever rose-colored glasses Angelica wore concerning her visit to the hotel, she had no problem spilling her secrets. Best to let her do it.

"Did anything interesting happen, with that sex magic?" Emberly asked, her tone conspiratorial. "Between us girls."

"I bet you'd like one of Grant's books," Angelica said. "This is what you really came for, isn't it? Not academia. You're looking to become a practitioner."

"Well, you know." Emberly swallowed, hoping an echo of Angelica's speech would endear her.

"The old ways never truly die. They sometimes fall out of fashion, but we're in a nostalgic time. Ancient devils, new gods." Angelica grinned again. She might have been attractive in a different way in her youth, but there was still a handsome woman tucked within Grant's robe. Maybe her lover had used his magic to help her age gracefully.

"What was the sex magic like that night?" Emberly asked. "At Cranberry Cove."

"Well." Angelic crossed her legs, and then she crossed her wrists over one bony knee. "That was an odd one. I'd heard of Grant playing with this intention before, with other lovers, but I never really got to see it myself. Rumors had wings in our little club. These magicians, especially invoking chaos work, they're never entirely sure what's real or not, or if they can make a thing real through belief. Never even sure what's going to work, you know?"

Emberly gave a slight nod. She had no idea what Angelica meant.

And Angelica seemed to know it. She leaned from the enormous seat, her teeth once more gleaming. There was a primality to her features, to the room surrounding her. The cluttered edges hugged closer to her, a council formed of an elderly woman and the unsorted junk.

Except it wasn't junk. The symbols on the walls and papers, the unknown contents of the boxes—this house might overflow with the needed makings of Grant's chaos magic.

The candlelight flickered as Angelica spoke. "Sometimes it's about how badly you want it. We don't know our hearts as much as we think." Her grin shoved at her sharp cheekbones. "We went upstairs, and Grant wanted to call a third into the hotel room. Someone who'd touch him while he touched me. The more, the merrier."

Emberly pursed her lips. She didn't want to ask

what kind of call Angelica meant. If the conversation died here, Emberly could invent her own ending to the story. That on the fateful night in Cranberry Cove, Grant had picked up the phone of whichever hotel room he and Angelica had holed up in and sent word downstairs to the Princes of Darkness convention that they would welcome one more into their bed. An eager third might have left the club and hurried upstairs to join the fun with Grant and his princess.

But Emberly hadn't heard Grant by the title of rotary dialer. She'd heard him by the title of summoner.

"Grant called him a kind of homunculus," Angelica said. "He was trying to make it make sense to me, and I'll be first to admit, I could be kind of a ditz when it came to the magic side with the Princes of Darkness. I was in it more for the companionship."

"A homunculus," Emberly said, and she forced out a tittering laugh. "I guess I'm a ditz about it, too. What does that mean?"

"It was like a vessel of willpower and magic," Angelica went on. "Those chaos sorcerers, they summon these things from—well, wherever they come from, you know? Beneath the world's skin. But it was shaped like a man, with the parts you'd expect from most men."

Emberly could have introduced Angelica to men of a different sort, but she kept her lips pursed so hard they hurt.

"And most importantly, he would do like you'd

expect a man to do." Angelica winked, and a shadow of decay crossed her face, as if she could only maintain flesh over her bones while Emberly sat fixed beneath twin blue eyes. "Spell-work is complicated, bits of wax and blood, intent and herbs. We spilled so much wax over that bed, but the hotel never charged us. Isn't that funny?"

Emberly flashed a wan smile.

"Mixing magics is like mixing drugs," Angelica said. "Never know what you're going to get out of it. An academic would want to test every possibility into an unquestionable graph, but it'd be pointless. Besides, where's the fun in that? Taking a wild thing like magic and taming it in a textbook. That's what I mean when I say, Grant was about the practice. Intent is sacred."

Emberly knew that much. In magic, and in many things.

"But there are constants, too," Angelica went on. "For a summoning, you got to have darkness. We had to douse the light in part of the room to give our man a way in, let him tear through from the underside. You need mystery for these sorts of things, shadows where the world's not so certain—how did Grant put it?" She snapped her fingers, her eyes brightening. "A liminality. Uncertainty and intent make the magic happen. And then the vessel can reach his fingers through the darkness and spread the world open, coming from his side to ours."

Angelica pressed open palms to either side of her, as if parting invisible curtains.

Emberly's fingers twitched for her bag, but she willed her hands to press down on her legs. Conner had somehow turned the electricity on at Cranberry Cove. If Angelica's ramblings had anything to do with the hotel and the guy-thing, at least Conner would be safe so long as the lights kept out the shadows.

THIRTEEN: BLINK

The ceiling light flickered over Room 2A, and Conner glanced to the window. Daylight had nudged through Cranberry Cove's glass in a gray haze, but it would make little difference against the room's dimness were the electricity to fail altogether.

Conner needed to move faster. He couldn't expect these lightbulbs to function for long. Unused as they might be, they were maybe a decade his senior. He wasn't going to think about the unnatural preservation of this place, as if the dust were an agent of cursed immortality that let the hotel age but never die. His arm-pasted nicotine patch itched, but he didn't want to rub it.

More than anything, he wanted a cigar. Badly. Probably his hardest craving in ten months. One sweet-smoked puff through his lips would make everything better. He resumed humming to give his mouth something to do.

The light flickered again. Conner marched toward

the door and flipped the wall switch up and down, forcing a dance of yellow bulbs and sun-broken shadow. Nothing breached those flashes of darkness to climb from under the beds or to reach through the holes Conner had broken in the walls. He quit flipping the switch, and the lightbulbs burned steady through the bedroom.

But not the bathroom. He had stepped in and out again, but he hadn't left its light on. The bathroom hung black and untouched.

Conner reached a hand around the corner and flipped the cold light switch.

On—a cramped bathroom of crumbly tiles and a too-fresh shower curtain. Maybe a recent visitor had brought it here with plans to squat in abandoned Cranberry Cove, only to disappear down the hotel's throat while midway through redecorating.

Off—absolute blackness filled the doorway and swallowed the end of Conner's arm.

On—Room 2A's bathroom again, ordinary and unimposing.

The frazzled sound of dying electricity caught Conner's ear. He leaned away from the bathroom and into the second-floor hall, keeping his shotgun hidden behind the doorframe from any fellow intruders who might have come fucking with the lights.

A bulb had gone dark in the hallway ceiling between Room 2G and Room 2H. The far end of the second-floor hall now hid in shadows, carving a line across the ratty carpet as if opening a space between two worlds.

"Em, you there?" Conner asked. "You're under orders to keep away from here."

No answer.

"Em? That you?" Conner switched off the shotgun's safety and eased his finger toward the trigger guard. "Anybody else?"

Still no answer. Conner's ears twitched at the silence. The hotel's stagnant air seemed to push out all sound, even the distance noises of town or natural airy ambience, as if the world beyond its walls had died since dawn.

Conner started humming again, and then his lips moved to half-remembered lyrics. Yes, he knew this song, had nodded along to it when it thumped from his car radio this morning. "Somebody's Watching Me." Like a deep root in Conner's mind meant to warn him about Cranberry Cove, and it was right to try.

He eased back into Room 2A and watched the ceiling light again for a flicker, a blink, any chance it might look at him wrong. The bulbs burned pale and endless. He reached for his phone and texted Emberly again. She would want to know he was okay.

But was he okay? He liked to think so, but there was no certainty in this miserable hotel.

He tested the bathroom's light one more time—it held steady—and then he marched inside and rammed his shotgun's stock against the wall with a harsh crack.

"Come out, come out, wherever you are," Conner sang. Maybe his instinct sensed ghosts, maybe unwanted eyes.

But either way, he had the feeling he wasn't alone.

FOURTEEN: MAGIC MAN

Emberly's bag thrummed. Another text from Conner, she guessed, but she couldn't check her phone now.

She lifted her coffee mug and pretended again to sip. "If I'm understanding right," she said. "The Princes of Darkness named you princess that night at Cranberry Cove. Which meant everyone wanted you, and Grant was special."

"Oh yeah, that night he was like a sorcerer king to the rest," Angelica said.

"You went upstairs to have a good time," Emberly went on. "And Grant wanted to have a better time, so he started this—" She swallowed hard, needing the right word. "Grant summoned more company. So, why do you say you never really got to see it? The—" She almost said *guy-thing*, and the rest of her question floundered on her tongue.

Angelica slipped in. "The sex magic vessel?" She let out a wistful sigh. "I would've loved to. Grant had fun plans in mind for himself, me, and our magic man.

But Hob, or Bob, whichever he was—the one who wanted me? He somehow got the key to our room and muscled in on us. That man was such a jealous prick, you know? Wouldn't have remembered him if it weren't the night I met Grant, but yeah, the two of them started brawling right there in the room."

"Over you?" Emberly tapped her lips. "I don't mean you wouldn't be worth it, but it's so—juvenile?"

"It was absolutely juvenile!" Angelica cackled, and her grin returned. "And pathetic too. For all that commotion, Hob-Bob lost the fight."

Emberly forced herself to smile back. "But I don't understand. Why didn't you get to see Grant's magic man?"

"How was I supposed to be in the mood anymore?" Angelica deflated against the back of her seat, and the titanic robe crumpled around her. "In that way, I suppose Hob-Bob won. He couldn't have me on account of my not wanting anything to do with him, but he spoiled our evening. The atmosphere was broken. Grant had been midway through the summoning and a little foreplay, but we were done. Still, he took my hand in his big mitt, and he kissed it, and then he kissed me, and then he took me out to dinner, away from the hotel. We ended up staying out all night. That was the last I saw of Cranberry Cove. Never went back."

A peaceful air settled over Angelica. She went still between the arms of her seat, as if telling the story had drained the last of her restless energy.

"But what about the guy-thing?" Emberly asked.

Angelica scrunched her face in confusion.

"The magic man. Your sex vessel." Emberly noticed her volume rising, but she couldn't rein it in. "Grant started the summoning. Wouldn't that thing still expect him?"

Angelica tittered. "How the hell should I know? He never knocked at the door. The magic man always knocks, that's what Grant said. A polite, courteous magic man."

Emberly thought of rhythmic knocking and clenched her teeth. "Polite."

"Honestly, I don't know if Grant even finished the spell," Angelica said, and then she wiped a hand over her eyes. "I was blindfolded. That helps with the liminality, or at least Grant said so. He might've been playing with me. Turn your back, shield your eyes, dim the lights. But then Hob-Bob burst in to ruin the fun, and I tore the blindfold off. No idea how far along Grant had got—I was never a magician." She gestured to the room of trinkets, candles, and the occult. "That was Grant's business. It's our home, but he's the one who knew about summoning. Best I could ever do was pretend to read a palm, and I only ever did that to fit in better with the Princes of Darkness."

"Is Grant here then?" Emberly asked. "I need someone who knows this weird shit."

Angelica half-laughed, half-sniffed. "He's always here. What, you want to meet him?"

Emberly said nothing, only set down her coffee mug and climbed from the couch with her bag latched over her shoulder. She'd known there was someone else here from the start. She could sense it in the air, and the air had tried to warn her too, rubbing her the wrong way, leaning the clutter of this house against her mind.

Angelica strained out of her chair—Grant's chair—and nudged through a gauntlet of cardboard boxes and strangely profane statues of Christ, with Emberly in tow. They were headed for the dark hallway she'd seen when first scanning the house. Paintings dotted its cream-colored walls, their imagery flashing uncertain eyes and streaks of red, each depicting hazy scenes of nakedness or violence as discomforting as *Saturn Devouring His Son*.

Emberly hurried to keep at Angelica's heels. She didn't want to walk alone in this hallway. It breathed Grant's liminality as if she could close her eyes, open them, and find herself somewhere entirely different.

"Could the magic man take people?" she asked. "Abduct them?"

Bony shoulders shrugged beneath Angelica's weighty robe. "I can't see why he'd bother. He was easy to satisfy, only wanted to do the job he'd been summoned for. That's the intent, and like I said, it's sacred."

They neared a dark, squarish door offset against the pale walls. Its mottled cracks spoke of medieval origins, somehow outlasting nations, plagues, and vast generations of mankind only to be dragged across oceans and set into the back of this tiny house. An iron ring hung from one side, its edges reddened with rust.

"Of course, Grant needed blood to call the vessel," Angelica said. She wrapped both hands around the ring and began to pull. Strained breath wheezed in and out between her lips. "I suppose the longer you. Kept him out. The more he'd need. But I can't imagine a disobedient vessel. Taking blood against the summoner's will."

"But if the summoner never went back," Emberly said. "What about then?"

Angelica glanced over her knotted shoulder. "You're a funny one. What are you saying?"

"Grant never went back." Emberly flinched to help Angelica with the door, but realization had turned her feet to lead. "If the vessel's only purpose was to touch him, and he never went back, then it couldn't finish his intent. And if it needed blood as part of the ritual, wouldn't it find blood? To keep itself going, so it could eventually do what Grant wanted?"

"Not sure," Angelica said. The door groaned open inch by scraping inch. "Like I told you, I was never much of a magician. It's really Grant's business."

Emberly would ask him then. Whether he was chatty like Angelica or needed persuading, Emberly would take everything he had to give. He'd already stolen the sense of a stable world from her. To believe a word on sex magic and the occult—it grated her thoughts, but what choice did she have?

Couldn't happen, so it didn't. Conner could think that way, but not Emberly. The impossible was ugly, present, and real. Everything added up.

Angelica finished dragging open the door and leaned against it. "Here," she said, panting shallow breaths. "Grant's room."

Emberly peered past her at a small round chamber, its walls built of thick stone blocks. Darkness opened between them in misshapen black slits. Unlike the rest of the house, there was no clutter on the floor, not one painting on the walls. The only source of light was an iron-barred window across from the open doorway, where sunshine streaked past the gray slate like a spotlight focused on the chamber's center.

On a gleaming brass urn, its front engraved with a name: *Grant Lodestar.*

Emberly's heart sank, but she stood firm as she stepped into the room. "How long ago?"

"Four years? Five?" Angelica pried herself from the wooden door. "Time gets strange at my age."

Emberly paused after two steps, between the doorway and the urn. The chamber's round shape distorted its size from the hallway, but from within it looked to be a little larger than a walk-in closet. Why keep Grant's urn in here and not in the living room brimming with his life's work?

"Now that we're here, I can't guess what Grant

would've told you," Angelica said, joining Emberly inside. "The intent is the important part, but everything else is a guess. He wouldn't have known it to a science—it was never science, you know? Maybe that's what he'd have told you. He never could get that spell to work that night, and never after either. It only sort of happened. You'll see what I mean."

"Will I?" Emberly glanced over her shoulder. "How do you know?"

"Because you're a seeker, and here's where Grant sought, too." Angelica raised an open palm to the curving stone wall, and a glint of sunshine caught in her pale eyes. "I've seen true chaos, girl. There are shadows in the slightest places, and mixing magics is uncertain work. Never know what you'll get. You can only put in the blood and the intent, and maybe a little luck. No such thing as a sure thing."

Emberly said nothing, but Angelica was off the mark. Grant's spell had worked. Had he and his princess stuck around the hotel back in 1976, they would've found out for themselves.

Now their vessel went snuffling through the dark walls of Cranberry Cove, hidden beneath the world's skin. Emberly imagined a man-shaped creature, lost for decades, determined to sate a summoner's lust, thirsting for blood to keep itself going, keep moving, keep alive to fulfill its sole purpose. It had mastered finding the dark passages of the hotel, its shadow places. At finding people who should never have come.

People who wouldn't be ready for Grant Lodestar's sex magic vessel to spread open the world and touch them. Take them, feed itself. Violate them in trying to fulfill its purpose. Try again, try again.

Except it would never succeed. Grant might have meant to summon the guy-thing from its world on other nights, but there was already a vessel, still determined to finish its last task from an autumn night in 1976.

It had never left Cranberry Cove.

"Couldn't he send it away?" Emberly asked. "Dismiss the magic man? Grant's gone, but you mentioned books. There has to be a way to send it home without finishing what it came to do."

"You really don't listen," Angelica said, laughing to herself. "I don't know magic, I told you that. It was all miracles to me. But at least I understood—the intent is sacred. You can't dismiss that intent. That's why it never fully worked later. Grant's heart wasn't in it here like it was at Cranberry Cove that night. And why would I bother him about it? You get a life like mine, where the world opens to arcane secrets, coughing up delights from the dark—you don't question a gift like that. Grant loved, and I loved, and you could have it anytime, any darkness."

"Even the magic man?" Emberly asked.

"Even the magic man. He could come from anywhere, whenever you needed, so long as he had shadows." Angelica managed another grin. "That's what made him magic."

Any darkness. Conner could pump all the electricity he liked into Cranberry Cove, but unless he burned it to the ground, he couldn't erase shadows from every place on every floor. There were always corners. There were undersides of beds, inside dresser drawers, holes in walls. Even that shadowy patch of the stairway landing.

Fingers would reach through those shadows and press aside the solid walls, easy as parting curtains, to let in something snuffling and terrible.

Emberly reached a hand into her bag. Her fingers traced something hard and cold, and at first she couldn't tell whether she touched her phone or her gun.

A fist rumpled her jacket between her shoulder blades and hauled her backward. She thumped hard against the wall, banging one elbow and shooting an ache down her arm. Cold stone breathed through her clothes, into her skin.

And something else breathed at her ear. She jerked forward, but her one arm snagged.

Another fist gripped the sleeve. A third hand tugged the waistline of her skirt, its fingernails scraping the small of her back. Yet another dug into her hair and yanked her scalp flush with the stone.

She cried out, tensing against grasping limbs and fingers, but they felt both heavy and yet a suggestion around her. These were conjured things, reaching out from the shadows and grasping anything they could touch. She couldn't find them as she pawed with her free hand. Couldn't turn her head to see them.

She could only see Angelica across the round chamber.

Her body stretched up the stone like ivy growing over the side of the house. She stood on tiptoes, arms extended, fingers splayed. All around her, the black slits between stone blocks had widened into gaping mouths, where the darkness danced and writhed as if alive, and Angelica writhed with it.

"Angelica," Emberly said in a panicked breath. "What are they?"

"It's like I can still feel my heart, reaching for me," Angelica said. A trembling sigh rattled up her throat. "My dear Grant."

Emberly struggled again, harder this time. Her sleeve tore loose from one fist, but it grabbed again, higher up her bicep, between arm and shoulder.

"Don't fuss," Angelica said, one sun-glinted eye glaring across the room. "They just need a moment to check if you're him. It's no big deal; they do it to me all the time. None of them can really see anything now, you know? Half-formed. They can't bring us in, and they can't get out, since the spell never really worked, like I told you. They won't hurt you."

But Angelica was wrong. The intent was different because she wanted it. Emberly did not, and they were hurting her in their fevered curiosity, their nails digging into her skin, their hands not understanding that she couldn't fit into the cracks in the walls with them. Each shadow writhed with desperation to complete an impossible task.

And they were all sniffing the air, or whispering, "Summoner. Grant. Where?"

Emberly couldn't look down with the fist gripping her hair, but she dove one hand into her bag and pawed inside again. Her fingertips inched along cold plastic—her phone—and then past that.

To her handgun.

She switched off the safety, shrugged her shoulders in an effort to shield her ears, and fired a round into the wall. The sound rocketed through her, needling a whine into one ear. She fired again anyway.

Both muzzle flares lit the world around her, and the fists let go of her hair, her skirt, her sleeve. She rushed two steps from the wall and turned, firing again, and again. Each gunshot cast another flare, briefly dispelling the darkness.

Emberly caught the flash of a gaunt face with nothing in the eyes.

And then the slits in the walls were narrow again, the stones in exactly the shape she'd found them when Angelica first opened the chamber door. Like nothing had happened.

Except something had. Emberly wouldn't pretend otherwise anymore.

"Stop it!" Angelica screeched, launching herself from the far wall. "Don't hurt them!"

Emberly didn't explain the half-formed vessels weren't hurt, only cowering from the light. She instead crashed her handgun across Angelica's jaw.

The impact thundered up Emberly's forearm as if she'd banged her elbow into the wall again.

Angelica was no chaos magician. She couldn't explain, and she couldn't help. She could only fall onto the stone floor in a crumpled heap, her lips spotted round with blood.

Emberly swept over her, into the chamber's center, and scooped up the brass urn.

Sniffing sounds echoed from every wall. Croaking whispers chased them, around and around the chamber like circling sharks, hungry for Emberly's prize.

"Summoner. Grant. Where?"

Emberly aimed her gun this way, that way, everywhere. Her free arm clutched the urn to her middle. She could no longer make out what had grabbed her and tried to drag her through the solid walls, but she could hear them, *feel* their breaths and voices.

They wanted Grant, here in the urn. Ashes might not be enough to sate the arcane intent he'd poured into them.

But ashes were better than nothing, and a far cry beyond what these conjured things had felt in years, groping desperately at Angelica, wishing for a Grant they couldn't find. Wishing for a form they would never have, a purpose they could never fulfill.

Emberly could try splashing them with ashes, and it might dismiss them. Their torment could end.

But they were trapped in these chamber walls. Couldn't get out, couldn't drag anyone in. At

Cranberry Cove, one of their fellow conjurations had run loose for decades. These ashes might be the only way to stop it. The only way to save Conner, prevent the street war. All of it.

Emberly darted over Angelica's prone figure. She didn't stop to check if Angelica was alive or dead, and right now, Emberly didn't care. The occult hellhole moaned around her as she barreled down the cursed hallway, through the cluttered living room, and out of the house.

The summer air was a relief to the oppressive indoor atmosphere, but there wasn't time to savor it.

Emberly hurried down the porch steps, juggling her handgun and phone between bag and hand, never letting go of the urn. Even when she dropped into the driver's seat, she kept it squeezed between her thighs. These were the only ashes of Grant Lodestar in the world. Emberly couldn't risk spilling them. The phone glowed with a waiting message.

CONNER: Still here, still good

It had arrived several minutes ago. Emberly tossed her bag into the Chrysler's passenger seat and then slid her thumb over her phone to tap out a frantic text.

And she hoped like hell that she wasn't too late.

FIFTEEN: WATCHING YOU

Conner was sitting on the toilet lid, staring at Room 2A's bathroom walls turned to Swiss cheese by his shotgun-turned-cudgel, when he realized he was humming "Somebody's Watching Me" again. A harmless song for other circumstances, but it had grown tiresome inside Cranberry Cove.

His forehead creased with the tension of rummaging in his mental jukebox for a more appropriate tune, and then he forced himself to hum "Every Breath You Take" instead.

Somebody was watching him? No, he would be watching them instead. He would turn the tables against the hotel's atmosphere and swing the morning into his favor.

Even as a confidence boost, he felt like he was losing his mind. He didn't want to give in to magical thinking, weird personifications, womanly concerns, but if he had no choice? If supernatural traces had already squirmed into the wrinkles of his brain? Then he would have to guess that a grim shadow of the world held sympathy for this sadistic hotel, either by man's will or through the same kind of existential malevolence as caused stillbirths, disease, and children with no choice but to cower in their own homes.

"Okay, world, you give your sympathies to the vicious," Conner said. "I'll give it to the rest."

He was about to resume humming, couldn't be sure which song, when his phone quaked from inside his jacket. It was Emberly—no surprise. She was destined to check back with him, same as he would have checked on her. Their mutual care formed a rubber band, malleable but tethering.

EMBERLY: get put

EMBERLY: get out get out

Conner pocketed the phone again and scoffed at the crater-broken walls. He'd expected a question like *How's the search going?* or even a message as short as *Any progress?* This order to leave—did she think she was Ricard? No, since Ricard believed in Conner's ability. Emberly had zero confidence in him.

He wasn't going to reply. Let her get her head on straight, remember how he could control a situation. He wouldn't let this get to him.

Knock-knock-knock.

He sat up too fast, shooting an ache down his lower back. His free hand helped cradle the shotgun, and he aimed toward the open bathroom doorway. The bedroom's light flickered again, but the bathroom's bulb held firm above him, casting a gun-toting shadow across the grimy tiles, unmarked by rodent feet.

There had been no signs of animals in Cranberry Cove. In the haze of summer heat, shouldn't mosquitos be swarming the damp spaces in the hotel?

Bats, rats, raccoons, ants, termites, gnats—none of it. Not a fucking housefly. Even the vermin knew better than to come here, but not Conner Bohme. What did that say about him?

"Get that crap out of your head," he muttered.

His shotgun nudged the bathroom door, and its hinges squealed until it tapped the doorframe. One shoe toed it shut. At the next sound of knocking, he would blast a hole through the door and tear through whichever shmuck thought it was a smart idea to sneak up on him in Room 2A. A gory red hole for Cranberry Cove.

He made to squeeze the shotgun trigger when his phone hummed again. His hands were full with the firearm. Aim the gun or answer the phone? He couldn't do both.

Conner eased the shotgun onto the sink's countertop, beside its porcelain edge. The barrel aimed away from the faucet, toward the shower curtain, and the basin's black drain stared up at him as he again rummaged his phone from his pocket.

EMBERLY: it comes from anywhere dark

EMBERLY: get out now

Zero confidence in him. His thumb slid over the screen to answer Emberly's texts, but what to type? Tell her again that he didn't believe in devils or ghosts? She already knew that.

"Don't say anything you'll regret," Conner said.

It was a warning he could have used countless times throughout his life. He especially didn't want to fuck up now. Not with her. He slid his thumb over the touchscreen's keyboard, intent on typing a quick *thank you* to let her know he appreciated the concern and that he cared about her too.

Knock-knock-knock.

Conner set the phone down hard on the sink's edge, snapped up the shotgun with both hands, and wheeled around. The sound hadn't come from the bathroom door, but from behind him.

He blinked. No, he must not have heard right, had to be confused. What he'd heard wasn't possible.

His shoes shuffled in careful inches toward the foot of the toilet. He pressed the shotgun's muzzle beneath the lid to pop it toward the tank. Sediment-strewn water filled the bowl, but he found no animal that might've banged its head against the lid's underside. Besides, what animal would bang three times in quick succession like that?

And again, what animals have you seen? Conner thought, gritting his teeth.

He let the lid clack shut. His sound direction had to be off, or he'd misheard the knocking earlier. And that was if he'd heard anything. How could he be certain when this hotel was giving him the creeps, when it had slipped ghosts into the heads of the people closest to him? He was starting to entertain the impossible, and if he did that, he would never come back.

There was no such thing as ghosts. Or devils, or boogeymen. A fist couldn't knock from inside a toilet.

His phone rumbled again. He leaned over to where it sat beside the sink basin. Another pair of texts glared up at him.

EMBERLY: get out Conner

EMBERLY: GET THE FUCK OUT

Conner let the phone sit where he'd left it and readied the shotgun again. Each of Emberly's texts had preceded the sound of knocking, and he had to be ready for whichever direction might bring the sound of rhythmic knuckles against a hard surface. The hidden passage was in this bathroom, somewhere. He only had to be ready to blow a hole in it, and all of Cranberry Cove's terrible secrets would come bleeding free.

The dangling shower curtain halfway covered the porcelain tub. Conner had shoved it aside to bash the wall open and then slid it back into place. Nothing could have danced in and out of his sight since then.

But nothing could have slipped out of the room when he came charging at Emberly's cries, either. The familiar panic went on ringing in his head. She might be shouting his name now from wherever she sat typing on her phone.

A vicious stranger might be skulking between the pipes, opening a hidden entrance from beneath the tub, above the shower, something Conner couldn't have known but would discover now.

He approached the shower, tension squeezing his limbs. One hand let the shotgun swing back and forth at his side, ready to ride his arm's momentum and aim again should he spot anyone standing in the tub.

His other hand reached for the shower curtain to yank it down for good. His fingers curled around the edges, crinkling the mildewy plastic around his fist. He readied to pull.

The bathroom inhaled behind him. A draft slid back from the shower curtain, teasing at its underside. Conner's clothes ruffled, trembling at the displaced air. His skin turned bumpy, and his neck hair stood on end, and his senses flared into full alarm, as if fingers far stronger than his shotgun had torn a fresh hole in the world. In the bathroom.

Knock-knock-knock.

Conner let go of the shower curtain, gripped the shotgun in both hands again, and charged for the toilet.

"That can't be!" He jammed the muzzle beneath the lid and shoved it up. "Where the hell are you?"

The draft once more sucked at him, the inhalation of a breach in the world opening wide behind him again.

He'd made a mistake, and yet he'd been right from the start. That knocking sound hadn't come from beneath the toilet lid.

It was the pipes beneath the sink.

He had no time to wheel around as a cold smothering hand latched across his face. An arm seized his middle like a constricting snake, and its hand gripped his side, beneath his jacket.

He let go of the shotgun with one hand and grasped at the thick fingers covering his face. They were fleshy and yet held an iron grip, locking his jaw and clamping his teeth, hurting his cheeks and nose. The bathroom light was a meek suggestion between them. He tried to turn around, aim the shotgun. Anything.

A pair of firm legs crossed over his from behind, drawing him backward. The entire body at his back was like a grasping hand. Pale light flickered in the bathroom ceiling, turning those silhouetted fingers into a dark blanket.

Conner was free. He was caught. He was backpedaling into a gaping maw.

The sink basin stretched out, and the drain gaped wide, the once-solid porcelain and steel morphing into whatever shape the shadows needed. The world gulped at the air and drank at Conner's body.

He tensed every muscle and pressed forward, but an anchor had him, dragging him back, back, and then down.

Into water and darkness.

The drain's throat widened as the grabbing thing threw its weight back, harder by the step.

Conner folded at the middle, where the arm coiled over his gut, and his thighs pressed against his chest. Screaming pain cracked through his lower spine.

He snapped one hand forward, clawing for a perch, a mercy, anything to grab onto and stop from dragging backward. His other hand squeezed and squeezed until it found resistance, where it pulled a familiar trigger.

A brief roar filled the bathroom. Conner's shotgun, shouting for help. The gunfire blasted a hole in the ceiling, and plaster rained over the tiles, but there was no one upstairs to notice his panic. No Emberly to hear him struggle.

He could scarcely make out the thrumming of his phone against a hard surface. Out of reach, as useless as his gun, and both phone and gun alike clattered to the floor tiles as his limbs folded around him and against each other. His broad form crushed and crunched, a small figure to be dragged down and down.

Only the gripping thing behind him had any control.

The sink basin and pipes closed around the light ahead as he barreled backward into the darkness. Into hidden places that were not passageways as he'd understood them. The solid world had parted like a curtain, and now those curtains were sweeping shut into firm plaster, porcelain, and steel.

He could make out a gray pipe in the spaces between the clutching fingers over his face, but all sight shrank the deeper he fell. Shadows swelled around his body as pressure beat across his spine, and at last, he understood.

The world was shutting its eye against him. It couldn't reach where he was going, and there was no point in ever looking at him again.

SIXTEEN: THE RETURN

Emberly pulled her Chrysler to the corner of Washington Avenue and Mayhew Street, bumper to bumper with Conner's gray Mazda. It hugged the curb at the intersection corner opposite the hotel, the same as two days ago, as if no time had passed.

Cranberry Cove, too, sat watchful, derelict, ignoring days and months and decades.

Emberly scrambled out of her car and had already passed the hood when she realized she hadn't shut the driver's door. She didn't head back. Her hand slapped Conner's window.

No one sat behind the wheel. She tried the door, but the car was locked up tight. Which meant he planned to step away from it for some time and wouldn't necessarily be coming right back. How long since he'd left it? Since he'd sent those first texts?

Emberly retreated a step into the vacant street and faced the opposite corner. One arm cradled the brass urn carrying Grant Lodestar's ashes, while her free hand pawed at her bag's innards, checking for her phone and handgun. She then crossed the intersection and headed inside the hotel.

Ladies first, Conner had said last time. She wished that would've been true today. Maybe she could've stopped him.

The hotel lobby stood silent around her. Why hadn't she noticed this unnatural quiet when she first stepped inside Cranberry Cove? Where there was life, there was sound, especially in the heat of summer. Clouds of gnats should be breathing out of the entrance, roaches should be thriving in the rot, and rats or mice should have chewed homes here.

But there was nothing. A hotel haunted by an unseen presence, and even the insects somehow knew to keep away.

Emberly could hardly make a dent in the soundscape. Her every footfall came muffled across the decayed lobby carpet. This was a place of stillness, raising a finger to its lips to hush her movements. It wanted her to stand here in silence, to decay at a crawl. These decades had eaten with decadent patience, and Emberly wondered if Grant Lodestar and his Princes of Darkness had woven spell-work into Cranberry Cove's walls, a kind of chaotic magical gratitude for sheltering their group that autumn night in 1976.

It sheltered pain now.

The loudest sound to ring through the hotel was the occasional metallic tap of Emberly's bag's clasp against the brass urn. A makeshift bell, announcing the master's return.

Emberly swallowed hard and added to the tinny noise. "Conner?"

No answer. If her voice couldn't pierce the spell of this tomb, why should Conner's? They might be calling for each other with no way to hear.

Emberly didn't find him in the lobby. The only signs of him again crossing paths with Cranberry Cove were the radiance in once-dormant lightbulbs and the new sets of footprints blemishing the dust. He hadn't gone rummaging for room keys, patrolling the pool area, or tossing tables in the dining room or convention hall, where the Princes of Darkness had chosen Angelica Glade as their princess decades ago. Why would he though?

It didn't happen down here, he'd said. *It happened up there.*

And he had only gone to his purpose upstairs. The fresh light had erased the shadows from the landing. Emberly took that for a hopeful omen as she ascended to the second floor.

"Are you here, Conner?" she called. "Give me a—"

She almost said to give her a sign, but she didn't want to invite that rhythmic knocking. It would come soon enough on its own.

The lobby had been left largely unbothered, but Room 2A was a disaster. Shifted furniture, scattered dust clumps, dark holes gaping in the walls like the needful slits in the chamber of Grant's ashes.

"Conner? Speak to me."

Emberly passed the shut bathroom door and checked under one bed, the other, even glanced into the black wall holes with her phone's flashlight, risking another glimpse of that gaunt face with hollow eyes. She shook the image out of her head. Unlikely that thought alone would summon the vessel, but however sacred Angelica thought intent might be, intent could be misread, ignored, disrespected, and her magic man did not ask the questions it should. It only asked desperately for its summoner.

"Conner, please."

Emberly returned to the bathroom door. Held her breath. Risked knocking. No answer.

"You in there?"

Still nothing. Emberly exhaled hard and grasped the doorknob. Held her breath again. Shoved the door open.

With the light glaring from the ceiling, the once-unsettling bathroom looked almost mundane. The shower curtain hung where Emberly remembered it. The sink and toilet appeared intact. Black holes opened the walls, but she couldn't be sure whether they had gaped here last time. She only knew for certain that what lay on the tile floor had not been there before.

Conner's shotgun. And next to it, Conner's phone. No blood, no hair.

No Conner.

Emberly stepped into the bathroom and sank to the

floor. Her eyes scanned the dark holes. Conner must have broken them open, either by shotgun blast or shotgun stock. He couldn't have known he'd created a dozen new entryways for a conjured vessel that walked and struck from shadows. And even without them, there were unseen places everywhere. You only needed somewhere you couldn't look.

"I can't—" Emberly trembled, cutting herself off. "He can't—"

She didn't know what to say. A refusal, a plea, an offer of bargaining to a disinterested reality, happy to shift its rules to not only make magic real but let it break the world around her. She thought again of the Crane poem about the universe. She used to judge its brief words as too optimistic, but maybe it had a point. Maybe the universe felt no obligation to mankind not out of indifference, but out of knowledge. Couldn't it be that man's assertion was incorrect? That the man, in his surety of his indisputable existence, was wrong?

And why should the universe bother with a man who didn't exist?

"Because he was my friend," Emberly whispered, her throat tightening. "Because he was good to me."

Doubtful the universe would ignore an assertion of the man's goodness. More likely, it would laugh and become the incarnate cruelty Emberly had believed in last night.

She kept searching for Conner anyway. Down the second-floor hallway, banging on doors, trying their knobs. Just in case he'd found a key after all, stepped inside, closed the door, needed a nap. Emberly had tolerated a dozen impossibilities made real today. She deserved an impossibility in her favor.

An hour passed as she wandered the hotel, peeping into fresh wall holes, chasing Conner's dust-breaking footprints to the third floor, the fourth—the highest floor he'd visited—checking the doors and banging on every surface she could find in case, in this universe or some netherworld, Conner could hear her and answer.

Knock-knock-knock.

Deep in her desperate violence, she couldn't be certain if she'd imagined the rhythmic knocking or somehow caught it beneath the racket. But she had a feeling it was the real deal, with a warning in the rhythm.

And worse, a promise that she was not going to find Conner. Something unnatural—a remnant of a chaos magician's old spell—had stretched the world open and crawled from Cranberry Cove's shadows to hurt Duke, inspect Emberly, and take Conner. The delights of the irresponsible from before Emberly and Conner were even born lasted long in this desolate place.

Now the guy-thing skulked some arcane darkness, snuffling beneath the thin skin of the mundane world. Always searching, never finding. Emberly's failure walked with it, lurking in her shadow cast by the lobby's stuttering lights as she descended the main stairway. A sign she had overstayed her welcome.

"I'm sorry, Conner." She rubbed her wrist under

her eyes, and then she raised her gun and fired it twice into the lobby's drooping ceiling. The muzzle flare might again dispel darkness.

There was a pause, and then the lights winked at Emberly. Cranberry Cove could play this game too, and she would run out of bullets long before the cursed hotel ran out of shadows. It would hold strong and malevolent so long as the vessel remained beneath its skin.

She had to put an end to it.

Knock-knock-knock.

She heard the rhythm clearly this time. The guy-thing wanted to know what she'd brought. She left the stairway and approached the center of the lobby's rug, where she switched on her handgun's safety and slid it into her bag. Both hands cupped the cold brass urn of Grant Lodestar.

Shadows thickened upon the landing above. Best to be quick now. Emberly didn't want to stay long enough to catch that vicious whisper again.

Summoner. Grant. Where?

"He's here!" Emberly shouted, her voice limp against the lobby's soft walls. "Summoner Grant. The one you wanted."

She hefted the urn and then placed it on the lobby's rug, unsettling the dust in a gentle gray cloud. The cold left her fingertips as she pried them loose and stood again. She listened for a series of fateful knocks. Nothing disturbed the hotel's suffocating quiet.

A vengeful temptation wriggled down her leg, the urge to kick at Grant's urn, spill his ashes over the rug, grind them down with her heel. Spit on them, piss on them, all kinder treatments than he deserved. He wanted to linger in this world? Leave his mess behind at Cranberry Cove? Might as well be his remains.

Her shoe nudged the urn's side, leaning it one way and then another.

But there was no point. Vindictiveness would not bring Conner back. Emberly could only try to mend someone else's mistake, and offering these ashen remains to the vessel of decades-old intent and much older sex magic might be the only way to relieve that vessel's purpose.

Grant's magic man. The magic man's Grant. Together at last.

"I'm giving him to you," Emberly said. "Grant Lodestar. The one you came for."

She listened again. Still nothing in the hotel. She wanted this place to be grateful, to hand Conner back to her in return for this chance of final death, but it remained stagnant. The guy-thing might be off in some shadow world, clutching onto Conner. Hurting him like it hurt Duke.

Or it might be listening. And waiting.

"Take Grant, and sort out what he brought you for." Emberly stepped away from the urn. "Finish the damn summoning, and never come back."

She wanted a sign that this offering would work.

Some promise that the pain and loss might at least put this curse to an end. No more assaults. No more disappearances.

But she couldn't prove a negative. At best, she could try to explain all this nonsense to Ricard and hope he would call off his street war before it started. He should instead pour money and influence into buying up this block and fortressing the hotel off from the rest of the world.

Better that than demolishing it or burning it down. Emberly didn't know this chaotic magic any better than Angelica. To destroy Cranberry Cove might risk freeing the guy-thing from the rubble.

The only ashes it should play in were the ones Emberly left behind.

She carried her bag to the hotel exit, where its open door squeaked against a light wind, breaking the stale summer air. Time to go. The streets here lay too quiet for comfort. They couldn't disguise a scrabbling in the flickering lobby behind her, or a clinking sound that might have been the brass lid lifting from an urn.

Or three familiar notes, polite and gentle, as they announced a presence rising from the darkness of Cranberry Cove.

Knock. Knock.

Knock.

ABOUT THE AUTHOR

HAILEY PIPER is the Bram Stoker Award-winning author of *Queen of Teeth*, *A Light Most Hateful*, *The Worm and His Kings*, and other books of dark fiction. She is an active member of the Horror Writers Association, with over 100 short stories appearing in *Weird Tales*, *Pseudopod*, *Cosmic Horror Monthly*, *The Hideous Book of Hidden Horrors* (also from Bad Hand Books), and other publications. Her non-fiction appears in *Writer's Digest*, *Library Journal*, *CrimeReads*, and elsewhere. Once hailing from the haunted woods of New York, she now lives with her wife in Maryland, where their occult rituals are secret.

Find Hailey at www.haileypiper.com.

Printed in the USA
CPSIA information can be obtained
at www.ICGtesting.com
JSHW080052200224
57558JS00002B/10